**Three couples . . .
Three stories . . .
One unforgettable night . . .
at the dance.**

THE GUYS:

Mason (gorgeous guy in gray sweater): Most popular, Most Athletic. Most everything . . . *except* for Most In Love With His Girlfriend, the other half of the Class Couple . . . his, um, date for the dance.

Michael (cutie in ski cap): As Class Clown, he asks his buddy Caroline (also Class Clown) to the big event as a *gag*. The whole night's a joke, right? So why is *she* taking it so seriously?

Claude (the shy European): A foreign exchange student from Belgium, he's flying home the morning after the dance. Which means *tonight* is his last chance to finally talk to the girl of his dreams. . . .

The Dance

CRAIG HILLMAN
KIERAN SCOTT
ELIZABETH SKURNICK

BANTAM BOOKS
NEW YORK · TORONTO · LONDON · SYDNEY · AUCKLAND

RL 6, age 12 and up

THE DANCE

A Bantam Book / December 1999

Cover photography by Michael Segal.

Produced by 17th Street Productions,
a division of Daniel Weiss Associates, Inc.
33 West 17th Street, New York, NY 10011.

ISBN: 0-553-49294-2

Published simultaneously in the United States and Canada

Bantam Books are published by Bantam Books, a division of Random
House, Inc. Its trademark, consisting of the words "Bantam Books" and
the portrayal of a rooster, is Registered in U.S. Patent and Trademark
Office and in other countries. Marca Registrada. Bantam Books, 1540
Broadway, New York, New York 10036.

PRINTED IN THE UNITED STATES OF AMERICA

OPM   0 9 8 7 6 5 4 3

Table of Contents

Mason & Erin   1

Michael & Caroline   75

Claude & Liza   157

Mason
& Erin

by
Kieran Scott

For Torin and Dylan

One

Erin Scott worked at warp speed, handing out flyers as she maneuvered through the crowded posthomeroom hallway of Riverside High. Someone slammed into her shoulder, sending her reeling, and she decided to take a breather. This campaigning stuff was more draining than she'd thought.

Unfortunately she stopped in front of a poster that read Cecily, Queen-to-be. Erin narrowed her eyes. Right smack in the center of the poster board was a blown-up picture of Cecily Vaughn, all blond and toothy.

"Queen-to-be," Erin muttered, hugging her stack of brightly colored flyers to her chest. "Not if I have anything to say about it."

Someone snatched a flyer from her hand. "*What* is this?"

"Hi, David," Erin said, turning around to face

3

her best friend. She knew David Everett was going to be more freaked out by this than anyone—most likely because he was the last to know. But one look at him told her he was even more surprised than she had anticipated. His freckled cheeks were actually flushed under his mop of shaggy brown hair. For the first time Erin's resolve faltered. If David wasn't behind her, maybe this wasn't the best idea.

"You want to be named queen of the winter formal?" he demanded, holding out the flyer he'd just taken from her as if she hadn't seen it. As if she hadn't spent the previous evening at Kinko's, watching the machines spit them out over and over.

"Hey! Look who can read!" Erin announced, patting David on the shoulder. Humor was always her best defense. She started down the hallway, thrusting papers left and right like a Xerox machine on hyperdrive and hoping he would just drop the subject. Not likely.

"When did this happen?" David asked, dodging the crowd to try to keep up with Erin's pace.

"It was a sudden brainstorm yesterday afternoon," Erin said over her shoulder, wishing he didn't sound *so* shocked.

"Well, you should've called me." David folded the paper and slipped it in his already overstuffed nylon backpack.

"Why? Would you have helped?" Erin asked skeptically.

"No. I would have smacked you upside the head," David said. He stopped next to his locker in the main hallway and had to practically flatten himself against the wall to avoid the steady stream of people.

Erin's heart fell. "That's why I didn't call you," she said. "And thanks for the support." She dropped the stack of flyers into David's arms and reached back to tighten her long, blond ponytail. Then she straightened her cable-knit sweater and took back the flyers, clutching them tightly. She didn't want him to see how his negativity affected her. If he did, he'd see an opening to talk her out of her plan, and she might let him. That couldn't happen. This was the best plan she'd had in ages.

"C'mon, Erin," David said, spinning his lock. "You can't be queen. You're a *sophomore*."

"So?" Erin asked, even though she knew herself that it was a long shot. "I know everyone."

"Doesn't matter," David said, frowning as he searched through his books.

Erin's face started to heat up. "I'm in all the clubs," she argued.

"Doesn't matter."

"I'm friendly, I'm okay to look at . . . and I'm smart!" Erin said, pointing a finger at him.

"Doesn't matter, doesn't matter, and . . . *really* doesn't matter," David said, grinning. He shoved some books in his bag, snapped it shut, and slammed his locker.

"All right. You're bringing me down here, Everett," Erin said, scowling at him. She thrust a flyer in the face of an unsuspecting freshman. "Why am I even friends with you?"

"'Cuz I'm charming in a really annoying sorta

way," David said with a lopsided smile that always made Erin smile back. "Look, I hate to be the reality check here, Scott," he said, throwing his arm around Erin's slim shoulders and steering her down the hall. "But there's a reason why no other girls are gunning for votes. And that reason's name is Cecily Vaughn—she's sure to win. Besides, the queen's *always* a senior. Usually the most superficially popular senior. You know, the one everyone's afraid of instead of the one everyone actually likes. Not only are you too young, but you're also too unintimidating."

"I can be mean," Erin said, noticing how sickeningly sweet her voice was. She'd have to do something about that.

David narrowed his brown eyes at her. "Why do you want to do this anyway? You never go in for popularity contests."

"Two words," Erin said, holding up a peace sign.

"Mason . . . Parker?" David asked with a grin, checking off one of her fingers, then the other.

"You know me too well." Erin laughed.

"It's a curse," David quipped. He stopped and pulled her over to the wall to get out of the flow of traffic. "Enlighten me. How is being queen going to help you snag the unsnaggable?"

"Okay, I know this sounds stupid," Erin said, leaning one shoulder against the cinder-block wall. "But Mason is definitely going to be king, right?"

"Mr. All-American, most likable, four-point-zero basketball center?" David shrugged. "I'd say he's got a shot."

"It's a lock. So if I win queen, he'll have to dance with me," Erin said. Just the thought of finding herself in Mason's arms sent her brain swimming.

David nodded knowingly and smiled. "I get it. And with the music and the ambiance and you in some big puffy dress, he'll just look into your eyes and realize you were meant for each other."

Erin sighed. "That's the idea anyway," she said, staring into space over his shoulder. She'd imagined the scenario a million times. She and Mason all decked out in formal wear, his beautiful brown eyes locked onto hers, his strong hands gently holding her waist . . . it had to happen. This unrequited-crush thing was getting really old.

"Keep dreamin'!" David grabbed the sleeve of her sweater and started down the hall again. Erin snapped out of her daydream just in time to avoid tripping over her own feet.

"Well, cynic boy," she said, yanking away her arm and trying to sound as confident as possible. She maneuvered away from him and walked ahead. "I'm not going to let you bring down my upwardly mobile spirits. I'm going to win this thing, and that's that. Whoever *wants* to be named Queen or King is allowed to let people know it. So that's all I'm doing."

Erin turned the corner into the B wing and froze, causing David to crash into her from behind. Mason was just coming out of the bathroom, and the sight of him snatched Erin's breath from her

7

throat. He was wearing an oatmeal-colored turtleneck sweater, and he looked like he'd just materialized from the pages of a J. Crew catalog.

Two of his friends walked out of the bathroom behind him, and they all started down the hall in Erin's direction. As they skimmed by, Mason glanced over and caught Erin's eye for a split second. But she was so embarrassed that he'd caught her staring, she looked away. She *always* looked away.

And then they were gone.

"Okay," David said, barely audible over the pounding of Erin's heart. "Now I understand why you can't just *ask* him to dance, since you obviously become mute when he's in your presence. . . ."

"Yeah?" Erin whimpered.

"But how are you going to get through a whole slow dance with him if you can't even look him in the eye?" David asked.

"Good question." Erin caught one last glimpse of Mason's broad back as he turned the corner. "But I'm gonna have to do it somehow."

They walked into their first-period class, and Erin handed out a few flyers as they made their way to their seats.

"So what's your plan for winning this thing?" David asked as Erin slid into her chair. "Good, old-fashioned, knee-soiling begging?"

"And if that doesn't work, there's always plan B," Erin said.

David plopped into the seat next to hers and raised one eyebrow. "Plan B?"

"Bribery," Erin explained with a smile.

"Why am I not surprised?" David chuckled as he shook his head. "So what am I, as your lowly date for the evening, supposed to do while you're off blackmailing people and dancing with Mr. Wonderful?"

Erin looked David right in the eye and smiled. "Well, I guess Cecily Vaughn will be needing a dance partner."

David laughed loudly as the bell rang to begin first period. "Yeah. That'll be the day."

"You can't break up with Cecily Vaughn on the day of the winter formal!" Nick DeLia said as he flung open the double doors of the stairwell on Friday afternoon.

Mason Parker followed Nick into the hallway, looking back over first one shoulder, then the other. "Could you say it a little louder, man? I don't think Cecily's one hundred and one friends heard you." Mason strolled over to a bank of vending machines and pulled a handful of change from the pocket of his corduroy pants. Nick leaned back against the wall next to him as Mason fed the change into a soda machine.

"What do you have, a death wish or something?" Nick asked in a slightly lower voice. "The girl *will* end you, you know. You were just named class couple."

"Look, I know she'll be upset, but I don't think she's going to be *that* upset," Mason said, punching

9

the button for a soda. He sighed as he bent down to retrieve the can. "Besides, I didn't say I was definitely doing it today. I just said I was thinking about doing it in general." Mason popped the top.

"Okay, but why?" Nick asked. "Cecily's *so* hot."

Mason looked into Nick's desperately confused face and couldn't help smiling. "Look, Cecily and I just sort of fell into this whole thing. We liked each other, we hooked up at Serena Waters's back-to-school party, and then five seconds later I blink, and we're class couple. I've been going out with the girl for three months, and I know almost nothing about her."

Mason sidestepped his friend and started down the hallway. A couple of girls giggled and blushed as he walked by, so Mason smiled at them politely—which only sent them into louder giggles. Sometimes Mason felt it was very weird to be him.

"What's to know?" Nick asked, loping along in his baggy jeans as he checked out Mason's admirers. "The girl's a babe. End of relevant facts."

Mason took a sip of his soda and shook his head. "And I wonder why you've never had a girlfriend."

"Whatever, man." Nick pulled off his baseball cap and put it on backward. "At least I'm smart enough to know you can't dump her on the day of the dance. That's cruel and unusual punishment."

"All right. I'm not going to do it today," Mason said. "There would be too much drama involved." He hooked the crushed can into a nearby garbage bin and started in on his lock. He knew he sounded like a heartless jerk, but everything he'd said about his relationship with Cecily was true. They never talked about anything deeper than her upcoming trip to France or his last basketball game. She was fun enough to hang out with, but so were half the girls in the school.

Mason had a feeling there was something more out there. In fact, he had a very solid feeling about a very specific someone. Someone who only had to walk into the room to stir up feelings that neither Cecily nor any other girl had ever come close to stirring. Someone who didn't giggle and swoon every time he walked by.

Staying in this relationship wasn't fair to him or to Cecily. Of course, he couldn't pour out all his feelings to Nick. He'd probably accuse Mason of watching too much Lifetime.

"I still don't get it, man," Nick said suddenly, staring at one of Cecily's Queen-to-be posters across the hall. "I mean, why would you give *that* up unless you had . . . Wait a minute." Nick's eyes were sparkling. "You've got someone else lined up, don't you?"

Mason slammed his locker shut. "No, I don't have someone else *lined up*." He sounded unconvincing even to himself.

"It's Chrissy Morrison, isn't it?" Nick said, ignoring Mason. "You and Chrissy."

"Chrissy?" Mason asked, shouldering his backpack. "I barely know her. I don't know if I've ever even really *talked* to her. Where did that come from?"

11

"I don't know. Did you *see* her in that miniskirt thing?" Nick asked.

Mason dropped his backpack onto the floor and put both hands on Nick's shoulders, looking him in the eye. "Listen to me carefully," he said, trying to use his deep brown eyes to break through to Nick's deeply buried conscience. It had to be in there some-where. "There is more to a girl than her body."

"I know that." Nick shrugged Mason off. He adjusted his jacket, then looked at Mason. "Like what?"

Mason fought hard to keep himself from crack-ing up. "Like if I had someone lined up," he began. "She would be smart and . . . active. Like, she'd be involved in clubs and stuff, and she'd be athletic. Plus she'd be funny and—"

"Hot," Nick said.

Mason thought about it for a second. "Cute," he said. "She doesn't have to be hot."

"You really do already have someone in mind." Nick grinned knowingly. "C'mon, spill. Who is it?"

Go ahead and tell him, Mason thought. *You know you want to know what he thinks.* He bent over to pick up his bag. "Erin Scott."

When Mason straightened up again, Nick was slack jawed. Mason felt his stomach turn. "You have *got* to be kidding me," Nick said, his hanging mouth shifting into a grin. He brought both hands to his head, leaned back, and hooted with laughter. "You are *so* dead. Torin is going to *kill* you!"

"Will you shut up?" Mason demanded. He

turned around and started off down the hall. Nick immediately fell into step with him.

"I'm sorry, man," Nick said, his voice filled with mirth. "But do you remember what Torin did when I told him I thought Erin was getting cute?"

"Yeah, yeah, yeah." Mason swallowed hard. "He flushed your face in the toilet until you promised never to go near her."

"Right!" Nick said triumphantly. "And you're his best friend. There's no way he's going to let you within ten *feet* of his little sister. He overheard her talking about kissing once and told her she wasn't allowed to watch *Party of Five* anymore. If she started dating an older guy . . . Plus he *knows* how far you've gone and who you've gone there with. There's no way—"

"Okay!" Mason stopped in the middle of the hall and held up his hands. "I know Torin's the protective older brother. But it's not like he's in charge of her. She can make her own decisions."

"Who are we talking about?"

Mason cleared his throat as Torin walked up behind him and slapped him on the back. His six-foot-four linebacker's build dwarfed even Mason.

"Nothing. No one," Mason said, sweat breaking out on his forehead. Nick just laughed.

At that moment someone shoved a pink flyer in Mason's face and he grabbed it away just in time to see David Everett, one of the guys from JV basketball, heading off down the hallway.

"What is this?" Mason asked, holding out the flyer.

"Oh . . . my . . . God," Torin said, grabbing the paper out of Mason's hands just as he finished reading the headline: Don't Follow the Lot—Vote for Scott!

Mason's heart started to pound in his ears. "Erin?" he asked, his brow knitting. "This isn't her style. I always thought your sister was above all that popularity crap."

Torin pushed his long, blond bangs out of his face and stared at the photocopied picture of Erin, smiling in her soccer uniform. Then he handed the flyer back to Mason. "And I always thought my sister was sane."

"Nice picture," Nick said, leaning over Mason's shoulder.

Torin narrowed his eyes at Nick, snatched away the paper, and crumpled it up in a ball. "Watch it," he said, pointing his index finger at Nick and leveling him with a warning glare.

"Oh yeah," Nick whispered gleefully to Mason as Torin whipped the flyer into a trash can. "You're dead."

Two

"TORIN! ARE YOU ever coming out of the bathroom, or have you finally become one with the mirror?"

Erin looked down at the gold watch she'd borrowed from her mother and frowned. "All I want is my hair spray. Can you just hand me my hair spray?"

The door popped open three inches, and Torin stuck her bottle of Pantene through the crack. She grabbed it, and he slammed the door again, leaving her with the scent of shaving cream and Speed Stick lingering in the air.

"Gee, thanks," Erin said sarcastically, wrinkling her nose. "What are you primping for anyway? You're only going with one of your friends."

The door swung wide, and a cloud of steam billowed out. When the moisture dispersed, Erin saw her brother standing in the middle of the bathroom, wearing nothing but his suit pants. His blond hair was slicked back, and half his face was covered with shaving cream.

"You're only going with one of your friends too, and you spent forty-five minutes on your eyelashes," Torin said. Then he bumped his forehead with the heel of his hand. "Oh! But I forgot! You're going to be crowned tonight," he added sarcastically. "I'd better cover myself up. I forgot I was in the presence of royalty."

"Hey! Stop picking on me about this," Erin said, smoothing the front of her black velvet gown. "Forty-five minutes is a huge exaggeration."

Torin went back to shaving but left the door open. "I don't get you, Erin." He pulled down on his cheek with one hand as he wielded the razor with the other.

"What's not to get?" Erin asked, leaning against the door frame. She held out her hands and inspected her nails. She'd never had a manicure until that afternoon, and her hands felt like they didn't belong on her body.

Torin looked at her looking at her fingers and smirked, so Erin tucked her hands under her arms. "You're always railing on about how contests like this are elitist and all that stuff," he said, swishing the razor through the water in the sink. "Why do you suddenly want to be named Most Elite?"

Erin rolled her eyes and checked her hair in the hallway mirror for the hundredth time, making sure none of the strands had fallen out of the complicated bun she'd spent days perfecting. "I don't want to be named Most Elite," she said. "I'm not doing this because I want attention."

"Well, you're definitely going to be getting a lot of attention in that dress," Torin said, rinsing his face.

"Ya think?" Erin asked, grinning and swinging the full skirt back and forth.

"You almost look like a girl," Torin joked, his blue eyes sparkling.

"Thanks a lot."

Torin patted himself dry and pulled on his shirt. "Okay, enough fooling around," he said, straightening his collar and yanking down on his cuffs. "I know why you're doing this whole campaign thing."

"Oh, really?" Erin said. She uncapped the hair spray and misted her hair. Then shook it up and sprayed again. At this point her hair was so solid, she was going to be keeping the upswept style until graduation.

"Yes, really." Torin coughed and waved his hand in the air. "I know you just want to get your hands on Mason."

Erin's heart dropped. She put the hair spray down on the hall table and crossed her arms over her chest. "That's so not true," she lied, feeling the color rise to her face.

"Oh, *please*," Torin said, mimicking her pose. "Don't even try it. You've had a crush on Mason ever since he let you watch horror movies with us when you were in the third grade."

"I do not," Erin denied, her blush deepening. She hated when Torin pulled his "I-know-everything" act. Of course, he pulled it ninety-nine percent of the

17

time, and he was almost always right. Torin stared her down until she caved.

"All right, I *do* have a crush on him," she said finally, returning her attention to her reflection so she wouldn't have to look him in the eye. She found an out-of-place hair and tucked it behind her ear. "But it hasn't been since the third grade. It's been since *you guys* were in the third grade and he showed me how to swim across the pool holding my breath the whole way."

"And you almost drowned?" Torin raised his eyebrows.

"And he pulled me out of the pool and wrapped a towel around me while you stood there and laughed," Erin recalled, her green eyes flashing. "He was even sweet in the third grade."

"He wasn't sweet," Torin said with a laugh. "He was afraid he was going to get spanked for almost killing you." He tucked in his shirt and went to work on his tie but gave up within five seconds.

Erin grinned and quit fussing with her hair. "Here, let me." She walked over to him and took the two ends of the tie.

"Why do you know how to do this and I don't?" Torin asked, tilting his head back in exasperation.

"Because when Dad tried to teach you, *I* was paying attention." Erin finished tying the knot and stepped back to admire her handiwork. "You look almost presentable," she said.

"Thanks," Torin answered, loosening the knot slightly. "Anyway, if you want to hang out with

Mason, why don't you just ask him to dance?"

Just the thought of walking up to Mason and putting herself on the line like that caused Erin's hands to shake.

"Right. In front of all your friends?" she said. "I can barely even get up the guts to talk to him when he's here hanging out with *you*." She paused and studied his face. "Why are you being so supportive about this anyway? Shouldn't you be locking me in my room at the thought of me with one of your friends?"

"Any other guy, yeah, I'd be freaking out," Torin said, fiddling with the buttons on his cuffs. "But Mason? You've got my blessing. I think you should just walk up to him, look him in the eye, and ask him to dance."

"Well, what if he said no?" Erin asked, looking at the floor.

"He wouldn't say no," Torin said matter-of-factly.

"Yeah?" Erin raised her eyebrows at him.

"Mason's a nice guy. He'd take pity on ya."

Erin felt her stomach turn. "Very funny," she said, narrowing her eyes. "So while I'm asking Mason to dance, why don't you finally tell him you're in love with his girlfriend?"

"It's not the same thing." Torin scowled. He turned around and walked into his room. Erin rolled her eyes and quickly straightened up the bathroom so their parents wouldn't lose it. Then she followed Torin—who was searching his cluttered bedroom floor for a pair of matching socks—and perched on the edge of his unmade bed.

"I know it's not the same thing," she said, picking lint off the skirt of her dress. Torin picked up a black sock, sniffed it, and tossed it over his shoulder. "But what it comes down to is we're both chicken. I can't even imagine going up to him with Cecily hovering and asking him to dance. She'd kill me."

Momentarily giving up on the sock search, Torin opened his closet. He inspected his tie in the full-length mirror. "You might not believe this," he said, glancing at her in the reflection, "but Cecily is not a raving lunatic. I think she can give up Mason for one dance."

"Whatever." Erin walked over to his dresser, dug through it, and found a pair of black dress socks mixed in with all the white ones. "The point is, I had to come up with another way to get to dance with Mason, and if I win . . . *when* I win, you'll have a chance at what you want too." She handed the socks to Torin.

He walked past her and sat down on the bed, pulling on the socks, and looked up at her skeptically. But as he studied her face, a wide grin started to break out on his own. "What are you planning?"

"Nothing," Erin said innocently, lacing her fingers together. "Just make sure you're there for Cecily when she comes looking."

At that moment Erin's father walked into the room, wearing his standard plaid shirt and jeans, camera in hand.

"You two look great," he said, grinning the older version of Torin's smile. "Come on. Get together."

He held his camera up to his eye, and Torin threw his arm over Erin's shoulders. Mr. Scott snapped the photo, temporarily blinding Erin.

"That's one for the mantel," Mr. Scott said. Erin smiled, glad that her roving-photographer father was here for her big night. It wouldn't have been the same without his monster professional camera equipment taking up half the living room.

"Dad, there's no more room on the mantel," Torin joked, rubbing his eyes.

Mr. Scott laughed. "I know. We'll just have to get rid of one of your football trophies."

"Ha, ha," Torin said.

"So, Erin, David's downstairs, and he's ready for his close-up," Mr. Scott informed her. "Let's go down and take some more pictures."

Erin took a deep breath to calm her fluttering nerves. What could possibly turn out to be the most important night of her life was about to begin. "Okay. I'm ready," she said. She started to follow her father out of the room.

"Hey, Erin," Torin said just as she was about to pass through the door. She looked back over her shoulder at him. "Good luck," he said. "I'm voting for you."

Erin grinned. "Thanks. And if this works out, you owe me big time."

"Wow! They did an amazing job!" Erin said breathlessly as she and David walked into the Riverside High cafeteria. The walls were all covered with black paper, and streamers and ribbons hung down from the ceiling, making the room look like a psychedelic jungle scene. Couples and intimate little crowds already dotted the room, and some of the braver souls were sporting loud, colorful Mardi Gras masks in keeping with the dance's theme. Confetti and glitter sparkled all over the floor. Riverside High's resident rock band, Xenophobic Linguistics, was setting up as a DJ spun warm-up tunes in the corner.

"Yeah," David said, shoving his hands into his pockets. "You'd almost never know that we get poisoned in this very room every day."

"Welcome! Happy Fat Tuesday!"

Erin instinctively clutched David's arm as the girl voted Most School Spirit, Serena Waters, came exploding out of the crowd like a clown on speed. She was wearing a gorgeous silver tank top with a long, satiny ice blue skirt and had a gaudy, feathered mask covering half her face. Her huge, pearly smile was covering the other half.

"Have you guys gotten your beads yet?" Serena asked, shaking her brown hair back from her shoulders.

"Beads?" David asked, backing up slightly.

"No. No, we haven't." Erin bowed her head to allow Serena to adorn her with the cheesy plastic beads, then laughed as David grabbed the girl's wrist to prevent her from accessorizing him.

Serena just handed him a set of yellow beads with her free hand and took off for the next unsuspecting dance goer. "Have fun!" she called out as she twirled away.

"Why are we here?" David muttered, wrapping the beads around his hand.

Erin scanned the room and picked out Mason instantly. Her heart skipped a dangerous number of beats. He was standing against the far wall with Cecily and her friends, wearing a perfectly cut black suit. Nick DeLia, who was standing to Mason's left, said something that made Mason laugh, and just the sight of his smile sent shivers down Erin's arms.

This has to work, Erin thought. *I have to win this thing.*

"We're here for him," she shouted over the music.

David followed her eyes and shook his head. "Don't drag me into your twisted love scheme," he said. "Besides, I don't think I'm Mason's type."

"Sorry." Erin grabbed David's hand. "Do you want to get something to eat?"

"You know eating's my favorite pastime," David said, glancing at the spread lining the back of the room and then smiling down at her. "But don't you want to get started on your bribery campaign?"

Erin patted her hair. "I think we're allowed to have a little fun first."

"Cool," David said. "Keep that attitude, and I just might get the JV basketball team on your bandwagon."

"Perfect." Erin wrapped her arm around David's with a smile. "Shockingly enough, most of them are already over there, chowing down."

Three

"AND THEN WE'RE going to spend *beaucoup* time on the Champs El-ee-zus," Cecily said, butchering the name of the most famous boulevard in Paris. "Mom says there's a ton of *très* chic shopping there."

Mason took a long sip of punch and scanned the cafeteria. A bunch of people were on the dance floor, but things were still pretty tame. It would take a little longer for everyone to loosen up and get out there. Cecily laughed, and Mason felt a sudden pang in the back of his neck. He reached his free hand back to rub his right shoulder. He wasn't sure if *he* was going to loosen up at all.

"So, what do *you* think, Mason?" Cecily's voice broke into his thoughts.

"I'm sorry. What were we talking about?" he asked, taking his gaze away from a piece of star-shaped glitter on the floor. Looking into her wide

24

blue eyes, he realized for the first time that she had found a dress that perfectly matched their color. She'd probably paid some staggering amount of cash to have it made.

"Serena's outfit," Cecily said, discreetly pointing out Serena Waters as she inspected the snack table. Her tank top was too sparkly, and her skirt was way too gauzy, but Mason's first impression was that it suited Serena's loud, boisterous personality perfectly. She looked great. Of course, he also knew that Cecily wasn't Serena's biggest fan, so she was probably looking for a negative assessment.

"She looks . . . interesting," Mason said.

Cecily and her friends, Akiko and Marni, all laughed. "That's a nice way of putting it," Cecily said. "It's no wonder she's deep in convo with the Trauther—I can't believe Tom Trauth wasn't named Biggest Nerd."

Mason felt the knot in his shoulder tighten. Whenever Cecily hung around with her friends, she instantly became about as shallow as a puddle. "Actually," Mason said, "I think she looks good. Even . . . pretty."

"Really?" Cecily's face reddened slightly as she flicked her eyes over Serena's outfit once more. "I guess it's okay."

"Yeah. I mean, it's not like she's on the bottom-five list," Marni said, twirling one of her brown tendril curls around her finger.

"What's the bottom-five list?" Mason asked, sure he didn't want to know.

"You know, the list of the five worst-dressed people at the dance," Akiko said, as if the bottom five was as much a tradition as the king and queen election.

Mason rolled his shoulders, feeling both sides tighten. "Tell me you have a top-five list," he said.

"Of course we do," Cecily said. She reached up and brushed some lint off his shoulder, smiling sympathetically. "We're not doing it to be mean," she whispered. "We're just bored."

Letting out a sigh, Mason slipped his arm around her waist. "If you're bored, let's go dance," he said, hoping that moving would calm him down. Getting out there on the loud, crowded dance floor would at least prevent them from talking with Marni and Akiko any longer.

But Cecily quickly moved away. "Just five more minutes," she said. "Chrissy Morrison isn't here yet, and I *really* want to see what she's wearing."

"Right. Well, I'll be over here if you need me." Mason pointed over his shoulder at the table behind them, where the girls had dropped their purses. He plopped down into a chair and let his shoulders slump, hoping the knots would start to unravel. Looking past Cecily and her friends, Mason stared blankly at the minglers across the room. He wondered if Erin was here yet. Wondered what she was wearing. Would it be long like Serena's or something that showed her legs? She'd probably look unbelievable in either. Mason felt his face flush just from thinking about her.

And then, like out of a dream, Erin walked into

his line of vision. She joined her date near the windows and spun around when one of her friends asked to see the back of her dress. She looked like a model. Her dark blond hair was pinned up in a twist, and her skin glistened smooth and silky in her black, strapless gown, which fell all the way to the floor.

He studied her as she laughed along with Dave. Normally Erin walked around in baggy sweaters and jeans and threw her hair back in a simple ponytail. Mason would have thought she'd be uncomfortable all dressed up, but she didn't look the least bit fazed. In fact, she looked completely confident and just plain gorgeous. Mason wasn't sure if he'd seen Erin in a dress since she used to put on ridiculous plays in the backyard, and the sight of her all dressed to kill was making his heart pound against his rib cage.

Mason glanced up at Cecily's back and stared. He wondered what she'd do if he asked a sophomore to dance. A sophomore who was running against her for queen, no less. She'd probably feel like he'd humiliated her in front of her friends. Somehow, knowing he was going to break up with her made him want to keep from hurting her in any other way. It was almost like he felt bad for her in advance.

And of course, Torin would pummel him. As marginally insane as Nick was, he had a point. Mason was going to have to go through Torin to get to Erin. Even if he just wanted to *dance* with her, he was going to have to deal with his best friend.

Mason closed his eyes and sighed. Why, of all people, did he have to develop a crush on Erin Scott?

Four

"COME ON, ROBYN," Erin prodded. "I'll do your biology homework for you."

Robyn Schaffer glanced around at her entourage, two of whom had the misfortune to have shown up in the same dress that Robyn wore, and rolled her eyes. "I already have Carrie do my biology homework," she said, smoothing her long, blond hair behind her ear.

"Carrie Vega?" David said with a laugh. "She probably thinks evolution is a new chain of clothing stores."

Robyn shot David a withering glare. "Did anyone ask for your input?"

Throwing up his hands in surrender, David took a step back. "That's my cue," he said. "I'll catch you later, E."

Erin wrapped her arms around herself and forced a smile. She didn't want him to leave, but she also couldn't blame him. He and Robyn had had a "thing" freshman year, and ever since they'd broken it off, they'd never been able to exchange more than two civil sentences. Of course, that probably had a lot to do with the fact that Robyn had made sure the breakup was as publicly humiliating as possible for David.

Instead of letting him down gently like any person who had a shred of a heart, Robyn had decided to make out with another guy in the middle of the crowded lobby. When David confronted her, Robyn had told him in the loudest, most condescending voice possible that she could no longer date a guy who kissed like a blowfish.

I can't believe I'm even talking to this person, Erin thought, feeling her blood rise as she remembered her best friend's devastation. But she'd started this, and she was going to finish it.

"I'll come find you," Erin told David.

"Yeah. Watch your back," David said under his breath. Then he looked at Robyn with a smirk. "I'm sorry to cut this lovely chat short," he said, "but there are some other people in the room who are actually worth talking to."

He strolled off casually, and Robyn's face turned red so fast, Erin braced herself for an explosion. But Robyn took a deep, loud breath through her nose and managed to bring down her level of redness to a dark pink.

"Okay, how about if I . . . give you my gym locker?" Erin suggested calmly. "Everyone wants my locker. It's all the way at the back of the locker room."

Robyn turned her sharp green eyes on Erin and smiled slyly. Erin had never met anyone else who could make a smile seem that void of warmth. "You know what you can do for me?" Robyn said, lifting her chin slightly. Erin saw her glance at the spot where David had been standing moments ago and felt a queasy stirring in her stomach.

"What?" Erin asked nervously.

"You can pants your little sidekick," Robyn said, sending her now subdued friends giggling around her.

"Yeah," her friend Deena—Robyn clone number one—chimed in. "I want to know if he wears boxers or briefs."

"No. Seriously," Erin said flatly.

"I'm totally serious," Robyn responded, rolling her shoulder blades back to bring herself up to full height. Erin wasn't impressed. She could take Robyn with both hands tied behind her back.

"Um, that would be a no," Erin said, staring Robyn in the eye.

"Then you won't get our votes." Robyn crossed her arms over her chest in haughty triumph. "That's my offer. Take it or leave it."

At that moment Mason walked by with Cecily, Nick, Torin, and their dates, heading toward the lobby. He had his head tilted down as he listened to something Nick was yelling in his ear, but as he passed by he looked up and caught Erin's eye. Erin smiled and almost looked away shyly as usual, but she somehow managed not to move for half a second. Mason actually smiled back. As an excited rush warmed Erin's skin, a perfect idea hit her like a bolt of lightning.

"I know!" Erin squealed, suddenly returning her attention to Robyn. She grabbed the girl's arm in the insincere way Robyn did to her so-called friends all the time. "How's this? What if I *don't* tell Mr. Foley that you cheat on every single one of his algebra quizzes?" she suggested, wide-eyed with fake excitement.

Robyn snatched her arm away. "You wouldn't."

"Try me," Erin said, feeling very Heather Locklear. "Vote for me, or you'll be doing 'A plus Bx equals C' all summer long."

"All right, fine," Robyn agreed. "I'll vote for you." She looked around at her friends. "We'll all vote for you."

Erin grinned. "Thanks!" she said triumphantly as she walked away. For once Robyn's power trip was going to work in Erin's favor. If Robyn really made all her followers vote for Erin, she was guaranteed the sophomore-lackey vote.

She turned around and searched the room for her next victim, rubbing her hands together giddily. First Mason had smiled at her and she'd somehow managed *not* to look away, and now she had Robyn Schaffer under her thumb. This was actually kind of fun.

"I just don't get it," Cecily said.

"What don't you get?" Mason asked, pulling at

his collar. He was standing slightly behind Cecily as they waited in the lobby to have their picture taken for the yearbook. Mason was starting to sweat. He couldn't believe he was going through with this. In a moment they'd be captured for eternity as class couple, and all he could think about was a nice way to let Cecily down gently.

"Well," Cecily began, crossing her arms in front of her as she looked across the lobby. "Did you ever notice that most of the couples at this school don't make any logical sense?"

Like us? Mason thought, feeling all his nerves go on alert. Did she know that he was planning to break up with her?

"Like who?" Mason asked as the photographer's bright flash went off. He watched as Serena and Mike Duncan, Most School Spirit, walked away from the fake marble background the photographer had brought with him. He and Cecily inched closer.

"Like, for example, what's the deal with Torin and Zoe?" Cecily asked.

Mason glanced across the room and saw Torin watching the proceedings with his date, Zoe Seiler. Torin lifted his chin at Mason and half smiled. He and Zoe were conversing, and they were standing sort of close together, but they didn't look like they were making a love connection. "You know Zoe and Torin just came as friends," Mason told Cecily.

"Yeah, but they have absolutely nothing in common," Cecily pointed out, turning around to face him. "She's a total brain. How can Torin spend the whole night with her when they have nothing to talk about?"

Exactly, Mason thought, trying desperately to keep from letting his confusion show on his face. *And how did we spend three months together when we have nothing to talk about?*

"It's just a dance," Mason said.

"Yeah, you're right," Cecily answered with a sigh. "I just don't think they go together. Not like—"

A chill worked its way down Mason's back. "Not like you and me?" he finished, swallowing hard.

Cecily blinked at him and then smiled slightly. "Well, we are class couple," she said as the flash went off again. "The public has spoken."

Mason tried to smile back, but he could barely breathe. It was so obvious that Cecily was proud of their class-couple status. How was it possible that they both had such different views of their relationship?

"Next!" the photographer called.

Cecily walked over and stood in front of the backdrop. Mason tried to follow, but when he moved his feet, he found that his legs were shaking and didn't want to work. *Just do it,* he told himself. *It's not that big a deal.*

"Now, *there's* a couple that makes sense," Cecily said with a little laugh as Mason joined her in front of the camera. Mason followed her gaze and saw Michael Redmont and Caroline Knapp engaged in an animated conversation as they waited to have their class-clown picture taken. Caroline burst out laughing, and Mason smiled.

Then his heart caught in his throat as a girl in a

33

long, black dress approached the couple. Erin. God, she looked so beautiful. He couldn't take this anymore. As soon as he was done with this stupid picture thing, he was going to have to talk to Torin. He glanced over at his best friend, but he was gone.

"Did Torin go back inside?" Mason asked as Cecily quickly powdered her nose.

She snapped the compact shut and glanced at him, her eyes wide. "I don't know. Why?" she asked, sounding oddly cold.

"I . . . uh . . . I just need to talk to him after this," Mason said, his brow furrowing. Why was she acting so schizo?

"About what? Why do you want to talk to him?" she asked, dropping her makeup back into her purse.

"Stuff," Mason said. "What's wrong with you?"

Cecily laughed, and Mason noticed she was slightly flushed. "Nothing. Just—nothing." She laid her purse aside and stepped back in front of the camera.

"Okay, you two," the beefy photographer said. "You're the couple, right? So look like a couple."

Cecily stepped closer to Mason, and he put his hand awkwardly on her waist.

"C'mon. You can do better than that," the photographer chided loudly.

Mason's eyes darted nervously in Erin's direction, but she hadn't looked up. For some reason, he didn't want her to see him and Cecily clutching each other for the camera.

Cecily threw her arms around Mason's neck. "What are you looking at?" she asked.

"Oh," Mason said, blushing. "I just saw Torin's little sister."

"Right. My *competition*," Cecily said. The condescending tone in her voice made his skin crawl.

"Do you have to say it like that?" Mason asked. He automatically wrapped his arms around Cecily's waist. Every fiber of his being just wanted to get this over with.

"What?" Cecily asked, her eyes wide again. "I think it's kind of sweet that she's running against me."

Whatever, Mason thought. His palms were sprouting little lakes of perspiration.

"Okay, smile!" the photographer ordered. Mason obeyed, and Cecily pressed closer to him as the flash went off.

The photographer moved away from the camera. "Beautiful!" he shouted. "Next!"

Mason followed Cecily as she headed back toward the cafeteria. They were going to have to walk right past Erin, who was now laughing along with Michael and Caroline, and Mason was preparing himself for the encounter when he stepped on Cecily's heel and deshoed her.

"Ow! Mason!" she complained, bending down to jam her heeled pump back on.

"Sorry, I didn't realize you'd stopped," Mason said.

Fiddling with her stocking, Cecily glanced over at Erin. "Why do you keep looking at her?" She pulled herself up straight. "Do you think she's pretty or something?"

More like perfect, actually, Mason thought.

35

"No . . . ," he answered. "I . . . uh . . . I was just spacing."

Cecily backed up slightly and looked him up and down. Then she crossed her slim arms over her stomach. "You can go . . . talk to her if you want," she told him warily.

Okay. And how about I ask her to dance while I'm over there? Mason thought. But his instincts told him that Cecily was just testing him and if he took her up on her offer, she was going to make a scene. He really didn't want to deal with that right now. Especially not in front of Erin.

"No. That's okay," he said. "Let's just go back inside."

Five

WHY DO THEY keep looking at me? Erin wondered as she watched Mason and Cecily from the corner of her eye. What if Cecily was mad at her for running against her or something? No. That was stupid. It wasn't like Cecily could possibly be intimidated by her. *They must be looking at Michael and Caroline,* she thought suddenly. She wasn't sure why they'd be doing that either, but that had to be it. There was no conceivable reason for her to be the subject of a conversation between Mason and Cecily. Back to the task at hand.

"So what do you guys think?" Erin asked Caroline and Michael when she sensed a break in their constant banter. She managed to rip her attention away from Mason for a moment. "Are you going to vote for me?"

"Sure," Caroline said. "I happen to know that most of the soccer team has already stuffed the ballot box for you. You know our teammates—down with the establishment!" she said, making a little fist.

Erin laughed but stopped when she saw the mischievous glint in Michael's eyes. "What?" she asked hesitantly.

Michael put his hands on his hips and smirked. "I hear you're handing out favors in exchange for votes."

Uh-oh, Erin thought. She didn't even want to hear what Michael wanted from her. Knowing him, it would probably involve water balloons or Krazy Glue. "Don't believe everything you hear," she said hopefully.

"Oh no. You're not going to lowball me, Scott." Michael shook his head. "You owe me a favor anyway."

Erin placed her hands on her own hips. "Since when?" she asked, eyeing him skeptically.

"Since I betrayed my friendship with Torin in the fourth grade and helped you convince him that your mom was going to sell him to the circus."

"You did *what?*" Caroline exclaimed.

"Oh my God," Erin said, holding one hand flat against her stomach as she started to laugh. "I totally forgot about that!"

Michael was laughing now too, and Erin felt the need to explain to an obviously intrigued Caroline. "Torin had beheaded all my Barbie dolls, and I wanted to get him back," Erin began.

"So I told him I overheard his mom and dad talking about selling him to the circus because he was so bad," Michael put in, shrugging it off as if it were a completely logical story to tell.

Caroline put a hand over her mouth and gasped. "That's awful!" she said, but Erin could tell from the glint in her eyes that she was amused.

"I told him he was going to be in charge of . . . uh . . . *cleaning up* after the elephants," Erin said, cringing as she remembered what a horrible little kid she was.

"I think he hid in his tree house for five hours before we convinced him we were just kidding." Michael sounded proud of his accomplishment.

"He's still queasy when we mention the circus."

Caroline laughed, and Erin looked at Michael. "Okay. So what do I have to do to get you to vote for me?" she asked.

"Are you kidding me? I need some time to think about this," Michael said, rubbing his palms together. "This is an opportunity that can't be taken lightly."

"Whatever," Erin said, rolling her eyes. "Just don't think I'm going to be part of some wacky high-jinks mission. I will not be putting a whoopee cushion on Mr. Regan's chair."

Michael's jaw dropped as he feigned shock. "Please! Give me some credit. I moved beyond whoopee cushions in the seventh grade."

"Yeah. Now he's all the way up to hand buzzers," Caroline quipped.

"No. That's your department," Michael said, flashing Caroline a grin. "How about this?" he asked Erin. "You help me get Torin again, and you got my vote."

Erin narrowed her eyes. "I don't know. What do you want me to do to him?"

"Just . . ." Michael looked at the ceiling as if he was searching for the answer. Finally he snapped his fingers and smiled. "In the spring turn all his track socks pink right before the meet against Valley, and we have a deal."

Erin laughed and stuck out her hand. "That'll be classic," she said as Michael shook her hand, sealing the bargain.

"Then you've got my vote," Michael said.

"On the campaign trail?" a new voice interrupted.

Erin looked up to find Cecily hovering just to Caroline's left . . . and she was clutching Mason's hand. As her stomach started to turn, Erin felt all her confidence fly out the window. Just standing this close to Cecily with her perfect makeup and her right-out-of-the-pages-of-*Vogue* dress made Erin feel like she was five years old again. She was a little kid trying to play in a grown-up's game.

"Yeah," she said, finally finding her voice. "Since I started so late . . ." She trailed off and looked at Michael for help.

Luckily Michael instantly picked up on her desperation. "You'd better watch your back, Cecily," Michael said, crooking his arm around Erin's neck. "The dark horse over here is nipping at your heels."

Cecily eyed Erin and smiled. "I don't mind competition," she said. "I think it's really cool that you decided to go for it as a sophomore."

"Yeah, me too," Mason said.

"Thanks," Erin replied. Her gaze darted from

Cecily to Mason, who looked almost nervous. Erin was pretty sure she'd never seen Mason lose his cool in her life. *He probably really thinks I'm an idiot for running against her. He probably thinks there's no way I can win.*

"So, anyway," Cecily said. "Good luck . . . Erin, right?"

"Yep," Erin said, then grimaced. Yep? She sounded like her father. "You too," she added, hoping to cover.

Cecily bestowed one last smile on the little group and then walked away, tugging Mason along with her. As Erin watched them go, Mason turned around quickly and lifted his hand in a motionless wave.

Erin forced a smile, but inside she was crumbling. After the way Cecily was clinging to him, she had a distinct feeling that she wouldn't be seeing Mason for the rest of the night.

How could life be so unfair? She'd been dreaming about Mason ever since she stopped fantasizing about castles and ponies and moved on to boys. She cherished every small, in-passing conversation she'd ever had with him—in the kitchen, bumping into him outside Torin's room, answering the phone when he called. Even though she could almost never manage much more than "hi," she cherished them.

And all along she'd been forced to watch him date. Watch him take pictures with Torin and their friends for the junior prom. Watch him get into splash wars with his girlfriends in her very own swimming pool.

41

All she wanted was one dance. That was all she was asking for. But thanks to Cecily Vaughn, she wasn't going to get it.

Unless I win, Erin thought, glaring at Cecily's retreating back. *I have to win.*

Mason was still trying to figure out Cecily's motivations for being nice to Erin as he opened the back door of the cafeteria. Was it some kind of psych-out strategy, or had she suddenly dropped her inborn competitive side and decided to actually be nice? A cold blast of air hit his face, temporarily knocking the wind out of him, and thoughts of Cecily disappeared. He kept one leg inside the warmth of the cafeteria and held open the door. There were a few obviously insane smokers standing around, sneaking cigarettes.

"Hey," he said, trying to catch the attention of Liza Wilde and the foreign-exchange student whose name he could never remember. They were sitting close to each other on the ground. "Have you guys seen Nick DeLia or Torin Scott?" he asked.

"In the corner," Liza said, gesturing over her shoulder.

"Thanks." Mason let the door slam behind him and tucked his hands under his armpits to keep them warm. He squinted as he approached the dark form in the corner. The outline of Nick's coat was visible, but he wasn't alone. There was someone else wrapped up in his coat with him.

"Nick?" Mason asked, freezing in his tracks.

Nick and his friend sprang apart, and Mason's eyes widened. Chrissy Morrison? It was all Mason could do to keep his mouth from dropping open.

"Hey, Chrissy," Mason said, nodding.

"Hey," Chrissy responded, cuddling back into Nick's arms. "You scared me."

Nick was grinning stupidly, and his eyes seemed glazed over. *And why not?* Mason thought. It was like one of the kid's lifelong aspirations had finally been achieved. Of course, there was the little problem of the whereabouts of Nick and Chrissy's dates, but that was a conversation for another time. Besides, Mason's skin was frosting over.

"What's up, man?" Nick asked, still smiling.

"I was just looking for Torin," Mason said, glancing around. "Akiko said she thought she saw you guys come out here together."

"Sorry," Nick said. "He hasn't been out here." He pulled Chrissy closer, and she giggled. "You still gonna talk to him about . . . ya know?" Nick asked him.

"Yeah," Mason said, backing up slightly. "Maybe I do have a death wish." He looked from Chrissy's face to Nick's and back again. They both looked blissfully happy. Maybe Nick had finally found himself a potential girlfriend. Cool. "You kids have fun," Mason said as he turned to walk off.

"Hey, Mason," Chrissy called.

He glanced over his shoulder.

"I just realized I saw Torin, like, five minutes ago," she said. "He and Cecily were inside talking about . . . I don't know. . . . It had something to do with the hotel in France."

Mason laughed. "Thanks, Chrissy. If Cecily was telling him about that, he'll be getting his ear talked off for the next fifteen minutes."

"Just enough time for you and Erin to get in a dance with no one noticing?" Nick asked, raising his eyebrows.

"Now you're catching on," Mason said, striding over to the door and swinging it open.

"Good luck!" Nick called.

The door slammed behind Mason, shutting out the smoke and freezing air, but his shirt was still crisp and cold against his skin. He moved along the wall until he had a good view of his friends' table. Sure enough, Cecily and Torin were sitting there together and Cecily was chatting up a storm. Her hands were in full-on gesture mode and Torin was leaning across the table a bit so he could hear her over the music.

What a trooper, Mason thought with a smile. He couldn't imagine that Torin was very interested in the details of the riverside inn Cecily had been talking about for the past two months, but his friend was definitely putting on a good show.

"Hey, Mason! What's up?" Michael Redmont said as he walked by, carefully balancing two cups of punch.

"Not much," Mason said. He was about to keep walking when he realized Michael was the last person he'd seen Erin with.

"Hey! Have you seen Erin Scott?" Mason asked.

The sooner he found her, the more likely he was to have time for that dance.

Michael grinned. "Yeah. She's over by the punch bowl, bribing the JV football team."

Mason stuffed his hands in his pockets. "What do you mean?" he asked.

"You haven't heard?" Michael began. "It's great. Erin wants to win this queen thing so bad, she's been running around giving out favors for votes all night. She's gonna play this supreme prank on Torin—"

Mason's stomach took a nosedive. "Wait a minute," he said. "You're serious?"

"Yeah. What's wrong?" Michael asked. "I think it's hysterical."

"Yeah," Mason said slowly. "Hysterical. I'll see you later, man."

Mason turned on his heel and kept along the same path, still looking for Erin but with a much more tentative step. He'd always thought it was odd but kind of cool that Erin was running for queen of the dance. Part of him thought she was doing it to be different—to show everyone that anyone could participate in these classically elitist things. He'd figured winning wasn't all that important to her.

But maybe he was wrong.

He stopped and scanned the dance floor distractedly. Could she really be *bribing* people? Was this contest really that important to her?

Was she somehow just as shallow as Cecily?

Six

"I STILL CAN'T believe you threatened Robyn."
David smiled as he handed Erin a cookie and
a napkin.

"It was great," Erin told him. "I just wish you
could've been there."

"Me too," David said through a mouthful of
food. "So who's your next victim?"

As Erin took a small bite of her snack, she saw
Tom Trauth scurrying by, favoring his right leg.

"Tom!" Erin called out.

The guy known as the Trauther looked startled
at the sound of his name but stopped and hobbled
over to her. His red hair was slightly ruffled, and his
face was flushed—as it almost always was.

"What's up, Erin . . . Dave?" Tom asked, glancing over his shoulder warily as if he was hiding from
someone.

"Hey, man," David said.

"Why are you pretending to limp?" Erin asked, looking down at Tom's bent left leg.

"Shhh!" Tom looked around, paranoid. Erin glanced at David's amused expression and had to bite the inside of her cheek to keep from laughing. "It's top secret."

"Ookay," Erin said, her brow furrowing. He was acting freaky, but she couldn't think of a time when Tom *hadn't* acted freaky. "Well, I just wanted to ask if you would vote for me for queen." She'd offer Tom something if she needed to, but they were friends from the Save the Earth club and she was pretty sure she could get his vote without shelling out any favors.

"Yeah. Yeah. Of course I will," Tom said, running a hand over his hair. "I think it's cool that you're running."

"Thanks," Erin replied, grinning. "Do you think the other guys from the computer club will vote for me?"

Tom sucked in air through his teeth, making a little hissing sound. Erin frowned. That didn't bode well. "I don't know," Tom said. "Those guys are all pretty much in love with Cecily. Some even have pictures of her from the yearbook as their screen savers."

"You're kidding," David said. "Can I get one of those?"

Erin whacked him on the shoulder.

"Kidding!" David exclaimed. He pushed his bangs out of his face, and they fell right back.

Tom shrugged. "Yes, it's sad but true. Most of

them use the one where she's doing that cheerleading jump." He paused and looked off into the distance doofily. "What a shot."

Erin shook her head and looked across the cafeteria at the table where Tom's friends had gathered. The guys were constructing a tower out of cups while the girls forlornly watched the dance floor. She could probably get the girls to vote for her by finding guys to slow dance with them, but what could she give the guys? It wasn't like she had five thousand megabytes of RAM in her beaded purse.

"Uh-oh. The wheels are turning," David said, taking a sip of his soda.

"What're you thinking?" Tom asked Erin, looking over his shoulder again.

"I'm trying to figure out how to bribe them," Erin said matter-of-factly.

Tom smirked. "Bribery. I like it." Then he snapped his fingers. "Don't you work at the movie theater downtown?" he asked.

"Yeah . . . " Erin answered.

Tom laid a hand on her back and turned to stand next to her, watching the little crowd of builders as they triumphantly topped off their tower. "All you gotta do," Tom said, "is tell those guys you'll get them in to see the next *Star Wars* episode on opening day, and they're yours."

"Brilliant," David announced with a grin. "I'll vote for you if you get me in there."

"You'll vote for me anyway," Erin said as a slow smile spread across her face. "Tom, you are a genius."

If I keep getting inside tips like this, I just might have a shot at this thing, she thought, her confidence building.

"Hey." He shrugged. "When it comes to the male psyche, I'm your man. Believe it or not, the Force is even more powerful than Cecily Vaughn."

Erin thanked Tom and determinedly dragged David across the room toward the now toppling cup tower. Hopefully the mystical force wasn't the only thing that could outpower Cecily.

Forget about what Michael said, Mason told himself as he made his way around the periphery of the dance floor. After all, it was Michael. Every other sentence out of his mouth was a joke. Erin wasn't fake. She wasn't shallow. She was the exact opposite. And that was why he was looking for her.

Mason spotted a group of Erin's friends and started to stroll over, studying the little crowd for a glimpse of Erin's blond hair or her perfect shoulders, but she wasn't there. Mason felt his nerves start to fray. Had she just disappeared the moment he had a chance to come find her?

Suddenly he heard a laugh, and he slowly turned around. There she was, sitting at a table in the corner, yucking it up with a crowd of guys who looked like rejects from an *X-Files* convention.

Those guys weren't part of her normal crowd. Mason felt the sickening squirm in his stomach again. What was she doing over there? Offering them dates in exchange for votes?

Realistically, Mason knew she didn't have a shot. The upperclassmen outnumbered the freshmen and sophomores, and there was no way the juniors and seniors were going to let the crown go to a lowly sophomore. It was sick that things like this mattered so much to people, but it was true.

Erin laughed again, and her whole face lit up. Her eyes squinted adorably, and it was like her skin glowed from within.

Mason couldn't hesitate a second longer. He wanted to talk to her and find out if being queen of the dance really mattered so much to her. He wanted to know for sure that she was the Erin he'd always admired and not a mini-Cecily. He took a deep breath and started toward the table.

"Mason."

Torin grabbed Mason's biceps, practically enclosing it with his unbelievably big hand. Mason's heart stopped.

"Hey, man," Mason said, quickly turning his back on Erin. Torin released his grip, and Mason yanked down on his sleeve to erase the handprint. "What's up?"

"I want to talk to you." Torin's expression was seriously serious. Mason had to concentrate to keep from backing away and completely betraying his guilt.

"Everything okay, man?" Mason asked, hoping against hope that he wasn't in for a confrontation with his best friend in the middle of a school dance.

"Yeah," Torin said, glancing to his left. He moved over a few steps to get away from the crowd, and Mason followed. His pulse was beginning to slow a bit. If this was about Erin, he'd probably already be dead. Maybe Torin had something else very pressing and sober to talk about in the middle of the biggest party of the year.

"You're freaking me out, here, T.," Mason said when they were a safe distance from the dance floor and any other peripheral conversations.

Torin looked at the floor and shoved his hands in the pockets of his dark blue pants. "We're friends, right?" he asked, glancing up at Mason.

"Right . . . ," Mason said slowly. Where was he going with this?

"And if there was something you thought I should know, you'd tell me, right?" Torin said.

"Uh . . . right," Mason answered. His heart was pounding again, and he felt his upper lip start to moisten with sweat. *Torin knew.* He knew Mason had a thing for his sister. Nick had told him, or he was psychic, or Cecily had mentioned Mason's staring in the lobby. Whatever. Mason was dead.

Torin looked him directly in the eye. "So, say you had something to tell me that you thought I wouldn't want to hear, but you thought I *should* hear it—you would tell me."

I am so dead, Mason thought. *Might as well just be a man and say it. He obviously already knows.* But he couldn't do it. Part of him was holding on to the hope that all of this was about a rip in the back of his pants or something.

"I'd tell you, T.," Mason said. He swallowed hard. "What is this all about anyway?"

Torin took a long breath and let it out audibly through his nose. He looked at Mason for a second as if he was sizing him up—mulling over whether or not Mason was telling the truth. "All right," he said. "You're not gonna like this—"

"Mason!"

Saved by Cecily.

She ran over and clutched his hand, completely out of breath. "There you are!" she said, her eyes darting between the two guys. "I've been looking all *over* for you!"

Mason's heart was still in his throat, but he somehow found his voice. "Yeah?"

"Yes!" she exclaimed, pulling on his arm. "Let's dance. I want to go dance. Now."

"Um. Okay," Mason said, throwing an apologetic look at Torin. "Duty calls," he said. "We'll do this later."

"Yeah," Torin said stonily. He stared after them, his face flushed as if he could barely hold in some boiling anger. Mason instinctively squeezed Cecily's hand, beyond thankful that she had swooped in when she had.

Now he had time to think of what to say when Torin confronted him again.

Seven

A S XENOPHOBIC LINGUISTICS brought their version of "Brown Eyed Girl" to an unusually noisy close, someone grabbed the microphone, causing a loud, piercing blast of feedback to echo off the cafeteria walls.

"Ugh!" David grunted, placing his hands over his ears. "I told you this room was reserved for torture."

Erin shook her head in a vain attempt to clear the ringing that had started in her eardrums and looked at the makeshift stage where the band was set up. Serena was standing up there, mask and all, clutching the microphone like it was an Oscar.

"Sorry about that, everyone!" she said loudly as another screech rang out from the speakers. "What's wrong with this thing?"

Leonard Katz, the bass player of the band, leaned into the mike and smiled. "It's a microphone, Serena," he said in a deep voice. "You don't have to yell."

Serena let out a short laugh. "Oh," she said. "Well, anyway, I just wanted to tell everyone that this is the last call for votes for the king and queen contest. Remember, your vote counts, so get up here and exercise your right to be heard!"

Trying to calm her fluttering heartbeat, Erin took a deep breath and leaned back into David. He reached up and put his hands on her shoulders.

"What's the matter, champ?" he asked, pressing his thumbs into her back. "You're not giving up on me now. Not after an evening of running around promising people brownies and baby-sitting services and sexual favors . . ."

Erin gasped and whirled around. "I did not!"

"Kidding!" David said, laughing as he backed away. "But it's good to see you're still awake."

"Jerk." Erin hit his arm. "Well, let's go vote."

"I already did," David said.

"Yeah?" Erin asked, glancing across the room as people crowded around the ornately decorated ballot box.

"Yeah, like, four times," David said.

Erin raised one eyebrow at him. "You're kidding again, right?"

"Of course. They check you off on a list when you vote," David told her with a grin. "But I would have voted at least four times if I could have."

"You know, you're not horrible to have around," Erin said, linking her arm with his.

David put his free hand over his heart. "Now you're making me blush."

Laughing, Erin led him over to the ballot box and grabbed one of the tiny slips of paper and a blunt pencil. Shakily she managed to print out her own name and then wrote out Mason's name beneath it. She looked at the paper for a moment, admiring the way their names looked together. Then David clicked his tongue and snatched the slip out of her hand. Erin watched, wishing for luck as David popped the folded paper through the slot.

"C'mon," David said, tugging her arm. "Let's go dance."

"Wait a minute," Erin said, her heart in her throat. She'd just caught a glimpse of Mason approaching the ballot box. "Just one sec."

Mason strolled over to the table in the casual way that Erin had come to recognize from about a mile away and picked up a piece of paper. She narrowed her eyes as some junior girl offered him her pencil with a flirtatious smile. Mason smiled back politely and thanked her. Then he leaned over the table and scrawled something on the paper.

When he straightened up, he looked right at Erin, and she held her breath. Then, unbelievably, he smiled. Every inch of Erin's skin was tingling as he walked over to the box and placed his vote in the slot. Then, even more unbelievably, he started weaving his way through the crowd toward her.

"Omigod," Erin said without moving her lips.

"Bet you would kill to know what was written on that paper," David whispered.

"Shut up." Erin's hands were shaking even more,

and she clutched them behind her, then in front of her, and then finally gave up and crossed her arms. By the time she was done with her impromptu fidgety fit, Mason was standing in front of them, hands in his pockets, hair just slightly tousled. Perfection.

Erin couldn't breathe. *Don't mess this up,* she warned herself.

"Hey, guys," Mason said.

"Hey, man," David answered.

"Hi!" Erin said, a bit too brightly.

"So, Erin . . . " Mason began.

Erin felt her heart respond with a heavy thud just from hearing him say her name and hoped her burning face wasn't too obvious under the dim lights. She felt David nudge her and realized it was her turn to speak. "So . . ."

"Listen," Mason said with a smile that made her shiver. "I know you put in a lot of time on this queen thing, and I just wanted to tell you . . ."

Erin's mind was racing ahead as she stared into the depths of his warm brown eyes. Maybe he wanted her to win. Maybe he was going to say, "Win or lose, I want you to know that I think you deserve to be queen."

Yeah. And then you woke up, Erin told herself.

"Win or lose," Mason started, and Erin held her breath. "Well, it doesn't really matter. These competitions mean nothing, you know? It's just a stupid popularity contest. No one's going to remember who won a year from now. I really hate the whole thing."

Oh my God, Erin thought. She almost reached

out to grip a table. He hadn't just said that. Not only did he think she wasn't going to win; he thought she'd just ridiculously wasted her time on a stupid popularity contest. *He must think I'm insane and shallow,* Erin thought desperately.

Mason was looking at her strangely, like he expected her to say something. But there were no words to describe what she was feeling. She'd made a complete fool out of herself.

"Anyway . . . good luck," Mason said finally.

"Right," she heard herself say.

"Well, I'll . . . um . . . I'll see you later." Mason turned and walked away.

"Right," she repeated.

As soon as he was out of earshot, Erin crumbled. "Oh no!" she said. "He thinks I'm an idiot! He thinks I'm a huge loser. A social-climbing poser." She put her hands over her face and willed herself to calm down. She had to keep her cool. She had to figure out how to make Mason realize she wasn't a freak who actually thought winning queen mattered.

"Wait a minute," David said, grabbing her wrists and pulling her hands away from her head. Erin looked into his face and just prayed he was going to tell her she'd imagined the whole thing.

"All I heard him do was wish you good luck."

"And nicely tell me he thought I had no chance," Erin corrected. "And tell me that he thought I'd put a lot of effort into something meaningless and insipid."

"I know he didn't use the word *insipid*," David quipped in an attempt at levity.

"Don't joke about this." Erin clutched her stomach. "I feel sick."

"Scott," David said. "In case you haven't noticed, Mason is a guy. No self-respecting guy actually cares about these things. Or if he did, he'd never admit it."

Erin glanced across the room, where Mason had already melted into the crowd. Maybe David was right. Maybe Mason didn't think she was a silly, superficial snob.

But what if he did?

Feeling queasy, Erin took a deep, shaky breath. "I think I have to go to the bathroom."

Erin took one last look at her pale reflection in the scratched surface of the bathroom mirror and squared her shoulders.

It's no big deal, she told herself over the dulled sound of dance music coming from the cafeteria outside. *Just suck it up and get back out there.* With a huge sigh, Erin yanked up on her strapless dress and walked out into the chaos.

Besides, she told herself, *you could still win, and then you'll get what you wanted all along. Then you'll have time to convince Mason you're not a loser.*

The music was suddenly cut dead, and Serena's voice sliced through the silence. Thankfully she managed to avoid the feedback this time.

"Okay, everyone, the votes have now been tallied!" Serena announced as Erin made her way from the end of the room back to the periphery of the dance floor. Her heart was skipping around inside her chest like it was playing ring-around-the-rosy. She noticed that her fingers had involuntarily crossed themselves.

I have to win. I have to win, Erin repeated to herself as she maneuvered her way to the front of the crowd. She apologized as she stepped on a few toes, but she was finally on the inner rim of the large circle that had already formed to make room for the king and queen. Serena was going off about what an honor it was to win the title, so Erin took a second to scan the faces all around her. Mason was nowhere to be found.

"Okay, everybody!" Serena said, taking a blue card from one of the chaperons. "Your King of the Winter Dance is . . ."

Erin's fingers crossed tighter.

"Mason Parker!" Serena announced.

A huge grin broke out across Erin's face as the crowd erupted in a round of applause. Again her gaze flitted quickly around the room, and then she saw him. He emerged from a group across the room with a breathtaking smile lighting up the entire dance floor. A few people hooted as he walked by and Mason ducked his head modestly.

Erin's heart was flying as he walked up to the stage and bent down so Serena could place the crown on his head. More than anything in the world, she wanted to be up there with him. And she could be, she realized. In moments she could be standing up there next to him. Maybe even holding his hand.

Desperately Erin scanned the room again, mentally

59

calculating the people whose votes she definitely had. Torin, Robyn and her friends, Caroline, Michael, Tom, Maya, Doug, David times four . . .

"And your queen is . . ."

Erin closed her eyes and crossed all her fingers. *Please, please, please!*

Serena sucked in an audible breath. "Cecily Vaughn!"

Every single nerve in Erin's body snapped, and she felt like she had nothing left to support her—to keep her from crumbling to the floor. Cecily stepped into the circle and moved across the floor so gracefully, she could have been gliding on ice. Erin felt her face go white. She could never move like that. Not if she'd practiced for weeks. She registered the fact that all the guys in the room were either gazing at Cecily appreciatively or glaring at Mason with envy.

This was it. She couldn't compete with that.

Erin let herself be tortured long enough to watch Mason take Cecily's hand and lead her onto the dance floor. She let her stomach turn as the band started to play a sweet, romantic song and Cecily moved fluidly into Mason's arms as if she belonged there.

The lights went down, the spotlight lit up, and Erin turned her back on the dance floor. It was time to find David, go home, and forget this night had ever happened.

Eight

MASON PUT HIS hands on Cecily's waist and blew out a loud breath as they started to sway to the slow guitar strains.

"So . . . we won," he said lamely.

"Yeah . . . we did," Cecily agreed, oddly sounding just as disinterested. Her hands rested lightly on his shoulders, and she was tapping her fingers against his jacket.

Mason's brow furrowed. "Are you okay?"

"I guess I'm just a little tired," Cecily said, gazing over his shoulder.

"Yeah. Me too," Mason answered. His words hung in the air as they continued to dance. Even with the music and the murmurings of the crowd, all Mason could hear was silence. Tense silence between himself and Cecily. This wasn't a normal romantic dance. There was something between them. She had to feel it too.

"Cecily—"

"Mason, there's something I have to tell you," she said, cutting him off. She pulled back slightly and looked him in the face. "I know this isn't the best moment, but I just . . . I just have to get it out."

Mason stopped hearing silence and started hearing his pulse. "Okay. What is it?"

"I think we need to break up," she said quickly, holding her breath at the end of the sentence.

"What?"

"I'm sorry. I just—"

"No, wait," Mason interrupted. He didn't want her to keep talking because she sounded so desperately upset and sorry. And she didn't need to be. In fact, his heart felt anything but sorrowful. "It's okay."

"It is?" Cecily asked, raising her perfect eyebrows. She looked slightly offended.

"No, not like that," he said, struggling to figure out how to explain himself. "I mean . . . I've just been thinking lately that this relationship hasn't really gone anywhere . . . right?"

Cecily shrugged. "We've just been kind of going along, and it doesn't really seem fair to—"

"To keep each other from . . . other things," Mason said, just on the edge of becoming giddy.

Cecily grinned. "Exactly!"

Mason felt like his spirits were dancing. He and Cecily lapsed into another silence, but this one was different. Now they were both light and happy . . . because they'd just broken up. This was one he hadn't heard of before.

"So, we are going to finish this dance, right?" Mason asked, scanning the crowd.

"Oh yeah," Cecily answered. "When have I ever given up the spotlight?" Mason laughed, and Cecily shook her head. "Hey. I'm capable of picking on myself."

Mason looked into her sparkling eyes. "Can I ask you something?"

"Sure," she said.

"When I said something about holding each other back from seeing other people, you seemed right on board. . . ." Cecily looked away as a slight blush rose to her cheeks. "Do you have someone else in mind?"

She looked up at him skeptically. "Promise not to freak out?"

"Promise," Mason said, holding up three fingers in the Boy Scout salute.

Cecily took a deep breath. "Okay . . . I kind of have a crush on Torin."

"Torin?" Mason said a bit too loudly. A few people on the edge of the circle looked up. "Sorry," he whispered.

"And he kind of likes me too," Cecily whispered back, ducking her head. "That's what he was going to tell you before when I interrupted you guys. I thought it would be better if I told you myself."

"You're kidding," Mason said. But then it hit him. Torin fully concentrating when Cecily was babbling about her trip. Torin asking if he and Mason were friends and if one of them knew something the other should know . . . Mason glanced around the crowd and finally found Torin. Torin glanced away the moment he saw Mason looking at him, but it was written all over his face. Torin was in love with Cecily. How could he have missed it?

"I don't believe it," Mason said blankly.

"Are you mad?" Cecily asked.

"No . . . ," Mason answered. He looked up at Torin again. "Well, yeah . . . a little." After all, his best friend *was* scamming on his girlfriend. But then again, he was scamming on his best friend's sister. Might be better to let bygones be bygones. "But you know what? You should dance with Torin after this."

Cecily smiled and squeezed his shoulders. "Yeah. I think I'll do that. What about you?" she prodded.

"Well, you spilled, so I guess I will too," Mason said. "Remember when you were asking me about Erin before?"

"Ha!" Cecily said, attracting a few more curious stares. "I knew it! You should be thanking me in advance for distracting Torin. He's going to lose it when he finds out you like her."

Mason chuckled, shaking his head. "Well, I'm not too sure of that anymore anyway. All that campaigning for votes and bribing people . . . I guess I thought she was different."

"Maybe I won't have to convince Torin to spare your life after all," Cecily told him as the last strains of the song faded away. "So . . . are we friends?"

"Friends," Mason agreed. He gave Cecily a quick kiss on the cheek as the cafeteria erupted in applause. He looked into her eyes, and they both smiled, then turned and walked to opposite sides of the room.

"Hey! Can I talk to you?"

Mason stopped halfway across the dance floor and turned to see if whoever was yelling was talking to him. Sure enough, David Everett emerged from the bustling partyers and walked right up to him.

"What's up, man?" Mason asked, bemused. The kid was all flushed and jumpy.

"Look, I only have a second," David said, glancing over his shoulder. "Erin will kill me if she sees me talking to you."

"What are you talking about?" Mason asked, intrigued. "Why does Erin care if you're talking to me?"

David actually rolled his eyes, and Mason felt his senses go on alert. It wasn't every day that some sophomore guy treated him like he was clueless.

"Look, man—," Mason began.

"No, you look," David said, holding out both hands as if he was trying to calm Mason down. "I can't believe I'm about to do this." He shook his head and stared at the glitter-covered floor for a moment, as if he was rethinking his plan.

"What?" Mason asked, starting to grow impatient.

"All right," David said, lifting his head to stare Mason in the eye. "Erin . . . likes you."

Mason drew back his head and felt a smile twitch at the side of his mouth before he even registered David's words. "She what?" he whispered.

"God! Isn't it obvious?" David said, throwing out his arms in exasperation. "Haven't you seen the way she looks at you?"

Shifting his weight from one foot to the other, Mason narrowed his eyes. He *had* noticed that every time he looked at Erin, she either didn't notice him or she looked away. She didn't giggle and fawn all over him like half the female population of the sophomore class.

"Look," David said. "The only reason she even wanted to win this whole queen thing was so that she could get a chance to dance with you."

"Seriously?" Mason asked, the furrow in his brow deepening. This evening was getting more and more bizarre by the second.

"Why do you *think* she went around bribing the entire student body?" David asked, his eyes wide. "Do you think she actually wants a stupid plastic crown?"

Mason grew so warm, he was sure his skin was about to melt off his body. "She did that for me?" he asked slowly. "She's not just gunning for popularity?"

David rolled his eyes again, and his jaw clenched. "Are you kidding me? Do you know *anything* about Erin?"

Taking a deep breath, Mason stuffed his hands in his pockets and found himself staring at David's scuffed shoes. The guy was right. How could he have given up on Erin that quickly? He should have known better.

"You know what? Just forget it," David told him. "You're not good enough for her. She just got burned twice, first by you, then by losing the one stupid chance she had for a dance."

He turned on his heel, but Mason grabbed his shoulder, forcing David to face him. "Wait a minute," Mason said. "This is just taking a second to process. You're telling me she only ran for queen so that she could be with me for one dance?"

David sighed loudly. "Yeah. And then you go over to her and tell her it doesn't matter. That it's just stupid. That you hate the whole thing. And now . . ." David paused and rubbed his hand over his face as if what he was about to say was so un-believable, he couldn't even believe it himself. "Can you imagine how she must feel right now?"

Heart in his throat, Mason studied David's face. "Are you kidding me with all this?"

David snorted a laugh. "That girl has been my best friend basically since birth. Why would I make this up?"

"Oh God," Mason whispered, suddenly feeling hollow inside. "I did do that, didn't I? I was just trying to let her know that it didn't really matter so that if she *lost* . . . she wouldn't feel so bad."

David shook his head. "Yeah, well, like I said, just imagine how she must feel at this exact moment."

Great, Mason thought. *The one thing I say to the girl all night, and I act like a total jerk. And then she loses the election.* Mason stared past David at the disco ball spinning in the center of the room. His head was spinning along with it. He'd spent the whole night chickening out of asking Erin to dance or making excuses for why he shouldn't do it. And all she'd done all night was campaign like a mad-woman so that she could get the opportunity to dance with him.

"Wait a minute," Mason said slowly. "If she wanted to dance with me, why didn't she just ask?"

David blew his bangs off his face and shrugged. "Chicks," he said. "They're complex."

Nine

Erin searched the crowd for David, swallowing back her heartache and forcing herself not to turn around and look at the dance floor. She knew she'd find Mason and Cecily wrapped up in a picture-perfect embrace, and there was no way her stomach could handle it.

"Where did he go?" Erin muttered to herself, knowing she looked like a crazy person, stalking the room and talking to herself. She didn't care. She just wanted to leave. "What is he, hiding from me or something?" David was probably afraid she'd be freaking out after losing. And maybe she was. But she wasn't going to take it out on him. In fact, she was already planning on taking it out on her pillow—if she could just find her date and get home.

"Hey, Erin!"

She turned around, using the back of her hand to quickly wipe a tear from her eye.

Tyrel Jackson and Bob Tolley were walking over to her, all grins. "So, we'll be getting that Spanish homework on Monday, right?" Tyrel asked. "I've got a pretty full weekend of channel surfing planned because of you."

Erin's eyes narrowed. "Spanish homework?" she asked, her head feeling foggy.

"Yeah," Bobby answered, slapping his hands together. "And can you put those colored sprinkles on my cupcakes?" He looked at Tyrel, obviously amused with himself. "I like sprinkles, don't you?"

"Love 'em," Tyrel answered, gleefully playing along.

"Wait a minute." Erin shook her head. "I didn't win."

"So?" Tyrel and Bobby asked in unison.

"So, the deal's off," Erin said, putting her hands on her hips. "All the deals are off."

Tyrel walked over to her and crooked his arm around her neck. "Not quite, my friend," he said. "The deal was, we get the stuff if we *vote* for you, not if you win. And we voted for you."

Erin felt the pit of her stomach turn into a lead ball that started to roll around in her insides. All those promises she'd made, and they'd gotten her nowhere. Her whole body started to go slack. "But—"

"Hey!" Bobby said. "A deal's a deal. Spanish homework and cupcakes. Don't back out on us now."

Erin took a deep breath as Tyrel released her. All she wanted to do was drop into a chair and just stay there and rot. She'd made a complete fool of herself. She'd practically begged the entire school to vote for her, which was so pathetic, it made her stomach turn. Then she'd lost anyway. And somehow in the process she'd managed to convince Mason that she was as shallow as a small puddle. Now she was going to spend the better part of a week baking, cleaning, writing out vocabulary lists, getting tickets, and baby-sitting other people's siblings.

She glanced morosely at Bobby and Tyrel. "Okay, you guys," she said weakly. "You're right. A deal's a deal."

Bobby and Tyrel high-fived triumphantly and took off, laughing. Erin was about to collapse and commence the wallowing stage of her misery, but suddenly she felt an arm slip around her back.

"I'll do the Spanish homework if you bake the cupcakes."

Erin's heart stopped. It couldn't be. That was Mason Parker's voice, but there was no possible way that Mason Parker had his arm around her right now. Before she could find the energy to turn her head and look, he had pulled his arm away and was standing in front of her. *Right* in front of her. She could see the slight stubble on his chin, smell his fabric softener. If she reached up, she could touch his lips.

"Hey," Mason said, smiling. "There's something I've been wanting to ask you all night."

What? Erin thought. *Why I'm such a loser?*

"Will you dance with me?" Mason asked, his chocolate brown eyes searching hers.

Erin was so shocked, she almost burst out crying. There was no way he actually wanted to dance with her. She briefly thought about pinching herself, but she didn't want to look like a freak. There had to be a reasonable explanation for this.

Mercy mission. That had to be it. Poor, pathetic Erin. She lost the big popularity contest, so he'd humor her by asking her to dance. Well, there was no way she was going to be pitied. Not even by Mason Park—

"Please?" Mason whispered.

Erin's heart melted. Pity was fine. She'd go in for a mercy dance—as long as she could get her noodle limbs to move.

"Okay," Erin said, surprised that her voice came out at all.

Mason held out his bent arm to her, and Erin slipped her own arm through it. Mason was holding his crown in his free hand, and as he led her through the slowly swaying dancers onto the dance floor, he reached up and placed it on her head. Erin could feel that it was crooked and too big, but she didn't care. It was Mason's. She guessed he meant it as a gesture of comfort, for trying.

Finding a semiopen area, Mason stopped and pulled Erin into his arms. She had a million questions floating around in her head, but all she could do was stare up at him. This was the most amazing moment she could ever have imagined. So much more amazing than being voted queen and winning a dance with Mason. He'd *asked* her. At that moment it didn't matter if he'd done it because he felt bad for her. She was in his arms, and that was all she cared about.

"So . . . Cecily and I decided to split up," Mason said.

"Really?" Erin asked, sounding like an excited child. She and Mason both laughed. "Sorry. I mean, that's too bad."

"No, it's not," Mason said. "We both had other things we needed to do."

"Oh," Erin said, confused. *What was that supposed to mean?* "Okay."

Mason reached up and gently straightened his crown on her head. "I . . . uh . . . I heard what you did . . . I mean . . . to dance with me," he said.

Erin felt her face turn fire-engine red, and she ended up staring directly at his tie. Oh God. It *was* a mercy dance. He was just humoring the silly little sophomore. She was never going to be able to face him again. Humiliated beyond belief, Erin started to pull away from him, but he tightened his grip on her back, causing her heart to respond with a thump.

"You could have just *asked* me to dance, you know," he said.

She was unable to look up. "Thanks. I'll remember that next time," she said.

"And I'm really sorry for what I said before by the ballot box," Mason continued. "I just—"

"You know what?" Erin said, finally finding her neck muscles along with her courage and looking him in the eye. "It doesn't matter. As far as I'm concerned, this whole night never happened. Not running for queen, not campaigning, not bribing everyone, not knowing that you know why I did it all . . ."

Mason smiled, lighting up his entire face—her face—the whole room. "Well, *one* thing happened," he said.

"What?" Erin asked, more confused than ever.

"This."

He leaned forward, looking into her eyes, and caught her lips with his. Stunned, Erin couldn't move for a moment, but then her eyes fluttered closed and she kissed him back. She'd been imagining this moment for years, but she'd never imagined such sweet, soft lips, or how perfect and gentle his hands would feel against her back, or how the loud guitar strains would just fade away into nothingness as every inch of her was focused on him.

When Mason finally pulled away, Erin opened her heavy eyelids and smiled. "Okay. *That* happened."

Michael
&
Caroline

by
Craig Hillman

For Kimberly

One

Friday, December 15
7:43 A.M.

CAROLINE KNAPP KNEW something was wrong the second she woke up.

One moment she'd been dreaming she was stuck in an elevator with Tom Cruise and Ricky Martin. The next moment she was wide awake, her blue-gray eyes focused on the wall beside her bed, her heart thumping in panic mode in her chest.

What had made her snap awake like that?

Caroline sat up in bed and glanced at her alarm clock. Then she grabbed it, pulling it close to her face and blinking at it in horror.

It was 7:44 A.M.!

In her entire seventeen-year existence, she'd never forgotten to set her alarm—until last night.

She had sixteen minutes to get to school.

Sixteen minutes meant she'd missed the bus nine minutes ago.

Sixteen minutes meant she didn't have time for a shower.

Caroline eyed her reflection in the mirror and groaned. Normally her shoulder-length, light brown hair was straight and looked okay. This morning it had decided to try the half-matted/half-fright-wig look. She plucked her softball cap off the grinning plastic skull on her dresser and plopped it on her head. After pulling on jeans, a waffle-knit, long-sleeved undershirt, and a gray hooded sweatshirt, Caroline stuck her feet in her Skechers, snatching up her cordless phone on her way out of her bedroom.

Fifteen minutes to go. And counting.

Why couldn't this have happened last week? Caroline griped to herself as she scurried along the upstairs hallway. Last week her parents would have been home and could have driven her to school. This week they were in Chicago—her dad to attend one of his boring medical seminars, her mother to shop and complain about the cold. They weren't due back until later that afternoon.

Caroline paused outside the closed door to her sister's room. Listening to Amy snore, Caroline debated whether to knock. Her sister, home on college break, *could* drive her to school, but the girl was a complete zombie first thing in the morning. Not to mention the fact that with her wedding just two weeks away, she could use all the beauty rest she could get.

Moving past Amy's room, Caroline clicked on the phone and punched in a number. As the line began to ring, she said a silent, hopeful prayer:

Please, let the Rat be home. . . .

7:45 A.M.

"Suzie's battery's dead," Michael Redmont announced as he entered the kitchen. Stomping his boots on the doormat, he pulled off his knit ski cap, ran a gloved hand over his short, thick brown hair, and then crossed to the wall phone.

The white-haired man seated at the breakfast table lowered the sports section of the newspaper, fixing the seventeen-year-old with his sharp, green-eyed gaze. "Aww, Mikey, you didn't forget to turn the headlights off, didja?"

Michael sighed. "Gee, Gramps. Now *that* would be the question you should've asked me last *night.*" His own green eyes flickered to the clock on the wall: 7:46.

Yikes.

He had precisely fourteen minutes to get to school—*if* he was lucky. Riverside High was a good eight to ten minutes away, and that was when the roads were clear of ice and rush-hour traffic. Since his mom had taken the car to her weeklong business conference, that left him with only one hope. Uncradling the phone receiver, he said a little prayer before dialing.

Please, let the Rat be home.

7, click, click, click, click, click, click, click.

5, click, click, click, click, click.

6, click, click, click, click, click, click.

C'mon, c'mon . . . Michael tapped his foot impatiently. He hated this phone, which by his estimate had been manufactured sometime in the Dark Ages. *I swear, it would be faster to send a letter.*

The truly ironic thing was, before his parents split up five years ago, before he and his mom moved to Ohio to live with her father, Michael hadn't even known rotary phones still *existed.* Honestly. The only ones he'd ever seen were on old TV shows. Then suddenly one day—*wham!*—not only did he find himself dialing phone numbers on actual *dials;* he was learning the hard way that life in his mom's childhood home could practically be an old TV show in itself.

His grandfather simply couldn't bring himself to get rid of something if it wasn't broken or if he thought there was some way he could repair it. Didn't matter what it was—a typewriter or a teacup. Gramps just took good care of his stuff. He knew how to make things work and how to *keep* them working. And *that* was the reason all the phones in his house still had dials, and *that* was why the toast was always burned on one side.

And, Michael thought as the phone line started ringing in his ear, *that was why he and Grandma stayed married for fifty-one years, right up until the day she passed away: because he could make it work. Unlike some other people I know . . .*

Gramps placed his paper down, drained his coffee mug, then slid his chair away from the table. "Don't you worry, Mikey," he said, hopping up with the agility of a man half his age. "I'll go get the jumper cables."

Michael put out his arm, barring the way to the garage door. "That's okay, Gramps. There's not enough time. And"—he gestured at his grandfather's outfit, a pair of light blue boxers and some tube socks—"you're in your underwear."

"How'd you know that?" chirped the receiver in Michael's hand.

"Oops—sorry, Rat," Michael said into the phone. "I was talking to Gramps."

You could always count on David "the Rat" Ratgartner to still be home at ten to eight on a school day. The Rat was a notoriously late sleeper.

"Listen, Rat, Suzie's on the fritz. You think you can give me a lift this morning?"

"No prob, Bob," the Rat responded. "As long as you don't mind a tight squeeze."

Michael's eyes widened curiously. "That all depends on who's doing the squeezing."

"Something for me to know and you to find out," came the mysterious response. "See you in a few, Stu."

Michael hung up the phone, then turned around to find his grandfather staring at him with his hands on his hips. "You *sure* you don't want a jump?" Gramps asked.

"Nah, that's okay. I'm getting a ride from my friend."

The white-haired man nodded, eyes narrowing. "You mean that gerbil fella?"

"Rat," Michael corrected.

"I coulda given you a lift."

Michael blinked. Was he hearing things correctly? "What—you mean in the *Duzer?* Yeah, *riiight.*"

The Duzer was his grandfather's pride and joy: a cream-colored 1936 Duesenberg with a gleaming chrome grille and all-leather interior. Unlike all the other relics his grandfather possessed, there was never any mystery as to why the Duzer was still up and running—it was practically in mint condition. In the over fifty years that his grandfather had owned it, it had barely been driven. In fact, in the five years that Michael had lived with Gramps, it hadn't been driven at all. The classic car remained parked in the garage, hidden under its custom-fitted lambskin tarp, month after month, all year long.

Gramps shrugged. "Hey—you never know. I might've said yes."

"Oh, come *on,*" Michael chided. "We both know you saying yes would be about as likely as *me* taking the bus to school."

His grandfather chuckled at that, shaking his head. "You know, that's something I'll never get about you kids today. What could possibly be so horrible about riding the bus?"

"What's so *horrible* about it?" Michael answered, making a face. "Gee, Gramps. It sure has been a long time since *you* were a senior in high school."

Gramps winked at Michael, green eyes sparkling. "I may be old, Mikey," he said, "but don't you forget: I can still lift my foot high enough to kick your scrawny butt. Watch this. . . ."

Gramps stretched his arms toward the ceiling, raised one knee above his waist, and stood there—in the middle of the kitchen—balancing on one foot and jiggling the other menacingly, like a geriatric kung fu fighter. "C'mon, tough stuff—you want a piece of me?"

Michael laughed. "Put on some clothes, Jackie Chan."

Two

7:54 A.M.

"YOU KNOW WHAT, Rat?" Caroline said. "Sometimes I get the sneaking suspicion that you care more about your drums than you do about your friends."

From the backseat Caroline watched her skinny driver's brown eyes peek at her in the rearview mirror. "That's not true," he answered, sounding slightly offended as he sped the beat-up Civic along Winding Valley Road.

"No? Then how do you explain that I'm sitting here, crammed in the back, while your bass drum is up front, wearing a seat belt?"

When the Rat had agreed to pick her up, he hadn't informed her she'd be sharing the ride with eight drums, four sets of cymbals, three mike stands, a pair of speakers, and a gym bag full of drumsticks, maracas, and a tambourine.

The Rat shrugged. "Hey," he replied, "I'm just protecting my investment. Believe me, if I'd spent twelve hundred bucks on you, *you'd* be the one behind the air bag."

Caroline chuckled. She always had fun kidding the Rat about his drums. They were one of the few things the long-haired senior was serious about.

For the past four years David Ratgartner had been the percussionist for Xenophobic Linguistics, which—according to their promotional flyer—was the Most Popular Rock Band in Riverside! What the flyer neglected to mention was that Xenophobic Linguistics was also the *only* rock band in Riverside. That had to be why the student council had asked them to perform at this year's winter formal.

Having live entertainment (instead of the usual DJ) wasn't the only thing that would be different about this year's dance, which was being held that very night in the school cafeteria. Whereas the last three winter formals shared similar, seasonal themes (namely, Winter Wonderland, Jingle-Bell Rock, and—Caroline's personal least favorite—The Blizzard of Ahhs), this year's motif was Mardi Gras Magic. Never mind the fact that the actual Mardi Gras was months away and on a Tuesday. At Riverside High it was being celebrated on Friday, December 15, from eight until midnight.

Caroline had never attended the winter formal before—and she had no intention of breaking that pattern tonight. For one thing, she wasn't sure her eardrums had fully recovered from Xenophobic

Linguistic's latest performance: the Xenopalooza Tour, a weeklong gig at the local bowling alley back in August.

For another, no one had asked her. Which was okay by her. Caroline knew she wasn't the "get-asked-to-the-dance" type. She was more one of the guys, a pal.

And besides, it's not like she had a crush on anyone anyway.

The Rat glanced over his shoulder. "Hey, Knapsack, you might want to squeeze over a bit."

Caroline looked beside her. The other two-thirds of the backseat was occupied by several drums in black leather cases, stacked on top of one another like large hatboxes. "What do you mean, 'squeeze over'?"

Instead of answering, the Rat tapped the brakes, edging the Honda toward the side of the road.

"Why are we stopping?" Caroline asked, but her words were drowned out as the Rat pressed a button, lowering the passenger-side window with a loud, mechanical hum. A blast of arctic air blew inside—followed closely by Michael Redmont's ski-capped head.

"Redmonster!" the Rat shouted at him.

"Ratman!" Michael shouted back. He peered in at all the drums, then his gaze landed on Caroline. His eyebrows shot up in surprise. "Hey, Knapsack."

Caroline nodded. "Hey, yourself."

Michael turned to the lanky driver. "Gee, Rat—looks like you got yourself a full boat here."

"Whaddaya mean? There's plenty of room." The Rat revved the motor. "Climb aboard, Mikey, my man. Time's a-wastin', and the Ratmobile is leaving the station!"

Michael looked hesitant, so Caroline added, "Hey, this is nothing—you should see all the guys he's got crammed in the trunk." Unlocking the door, she hefted her backpack off the floor and onto her lap, scooting over against the stack of drum cases to make some room. A second later Michael Redmont folded his six-foot frame onto the seat beside her, closing the door behind him with some difficulty.

As the Honda took off, Caroline and Michael shifted around, struggling in vain to get comfortable. It wasn't easy. After some squirming and elbow fencing, a final position was arrived at: They were now both tilted up on one hip, sort of facing each other, legs held out straight, arms pinned in between. It was far from comfortable but just about bearable.

"See?" the Rat said once they'd settled down. "I knew you'd both fit."

Caroline rolled her eyes. "Yeah—like a couple of square pegs," she muttered under her breath but loud enough for the Rat to hear.

"I was thinking sardines myself," Michael grumbled back, then flashed her a smile.

His eyes are green, Caroline observed, and wondered why she'd never noticed that before.

The simple answer was that they'd never had their faces so close together; as it was, the brim of her baseball cap was practically gouging his forehead.

But even so, was it really possible that she'd *never* noticed Michael's eye color until now? *Michael Redmont*, who she'd hung around with since freshman year? It didn't seem likely.

I mean, how could I not have noticed before, when his eyes are so—

She realized she was staring at him. Lowering her gaze, she pretended to study the backpack that was being crushed in between them.

And suddenly regretted not taking a shower.

7:58 A.M.

"I'm really, really, *really* sorry."

Michael cursed himself silently as the Rat steered his car into the senior parking lot.

Smooth move, Mikey.

In an attempt to make the ride more comfortable, he'd tried to maneuver his arm up and around Caroline Knapp's shoulders. *Tried* to.

"Hey—don't worry about it," she told him, rubbing her eye socket with the heel of her palm. "How's your elbow?"

"Attached to a major klutz, apparently." He bit his lip. "Are you *sure* you're all right?"

"I'll survive." Caroline smiled reassuringly and shrugged. "Besides, it's no big loss. I only used this eye to help the other one perceive depth."

The fact that she was joking should have made

him feel better, but it didn't. Caroline Knapp was *always* joking. On the one hand, her sense of humor was the main reason they were good friends. On the other hand, the constant jokes made it hard to tell when or if she was ever being serious underneath. For all he knew, he might've just given her a black eye.

The Rat slid the Honda into his assigned space, cutting the engine. "Looks like we made it," he announced, removing his keys and jerking on the parking brake.

Michael looked across the lot, where a dozen or so students were lingering outside the entrance to the school. That meant the one-minute bell hadn't rung yet. Michael relaxed a little.

The one-minute bell shrilled.

The three of them jumped out of the car and raced across the icy blacktop and into the single-story, redbrick building just in time to hear:

"*. . . now have one minute to report to homeroom.*"

The announcement boomed over the PA system, and all through the hallway lockers slammed, conversations were cut short, and students dashed to their designated classrooms.

The Rat and Michael were in the same homeroom, which was at the far end of the building. Caroline's homeroom was equally far but down a separate hall. At the intersection of the two corridors Caroline broke off from the two boys. The Rat ran on ahead, but Michael held back. He was still feeling pretty guilty about whacking Caroline in the eye. He followed her, calling out her name.

Already halfway down the corridor, Caroline slowed her jog slightly, glancing over her shoulder. "Yeah?" she called back.

His mind was suddenly blank. "Uhh . . . see you at lunch?"

What was wrong with him? It was a stupid question. Michael *always* saw Caroline at lunch. They sat at the same table.

Caroline looked at him funny, nodded, then hurried away.

Michael winced. Maybe being squished against her in the car had squished his brain too. Why else would he be suddenly all formal with the Knapsack?

Three

12:37 *P.M.*

"I DON'T KNOW who this Mardi Gras fella was, but he must've been one pretty important dude to get a big holiday named after him—don't ya think, Knapsack?"

Michael slid his lunch tray another few inches along the metal counter, waiting his turn at the cash register. Standing in line behind him, Caroline reached for a veggie burger.

"Oh, don't be stupid, Mikey," she chided. "Mardi Gras isn't some *guy*. Everyone knows it's this huge party town somewhere in Louisiana."

Then they waited, together counting off the seconds: *"One . . . two . . . three . . ."*

Before they got to *four,* the person in line ahead of them spun around with a casual flip of her long blond hair. *"Actually,"* Cecily Vaughn told them, "you're *both* wrong."

Caroline and Michael shared a conspiratorial look: *Here it comes.*

Caroline knew there were two things Cecily Vaughn could never pass up: (1) any piece of clothing with a designer label in it and (2) an opportunity to show off her extensive knowledge of the French language. It was this latter habit that Michael and Caroline had converted into a daily game of theirs: the Let's-Get-Cecily-to-Say-Something-in-French-Today game.

"For your information," Cecily continued, "Mardi Gras is the French expression for 'Fat Tuesday.' It's a celebration that takes place on the eve of Lent, the forty-day period before Easter." She focused her blue eyes on Caroline. "I believe the 'huge party town' you're thinking of is *New Orleans,* where Mardi Gras is a big tourist attraction."

Cecily pronounced the city's name "Nawlins," as if to demonstrate the fact that she'd been there before and learned the proper way to say it.

"New Orleans?" Caroline repeated, purposely pronouncing it "New Or-*leens.*" (She had cousins in Louisiana, and they'd told her that the only people who ever said "Nawlins" were pretentious tourists.) "You don't say. . . ."

"Ah—*mais oui,*" Cecily replied, sliding her tray along.

Michael and Caroline grinned at each other. Licking the tip of her index finger, Caroline made an imaginary chalk mark in the air: *score.*

*   *   *

12:41 P.M.

"Omigod—did you hear? There's, like, some sophomore girl who's, like, *campaigning* to be elected queen of the dance." Robyn Schaffer paused to eat a spoonful of yogurt. "Can you, like, believe it?"

The group of senior girls sitting around her snickered and shook their heads.

"No *way*," Pattye Grecko replied. "I mean, like, how desperate can you, like, get?"

Sitting at the far end of the table, Caroline leaned over to Michael. "I, like, totally have, like, no, like, idea," she whispered in his ear.

Michael stifled a laugh. He and Caroline didn't normally eat at the same table with Robyn, Pattye, and their gaggle of giggling girlfriends, but today they'd had to. Their usual table was on the half of the cafeteria that the student council were currently in the process of decorating.

A bunch of students on ladders were busy covering the light green walls with giant sheets of black paper. Standing below them, three girls were inflating purple and gold balloons with helium from a large, hissing tank. Toward the center of the room a small stage had been set up against the wall for the band. The Rat's drum cases were piled on top, next to a bunch of sound equipment. In front of the platform some more students were measuring out lengths of purple and gold crepe-paper streamers on the floor.

Watching them work, Michael commented,

"Gee. Purple and gold. I wonder who decided *those* should be the official dance colors?"

Caroline thought a moment. "A kindergartner with no taste?"

Michael grinned. Across from him Dan Futterman was sitting next to Bennett Lee. They were two more transplantees from Michael and Caroline's regular table. "What's wrong with purple and gold?" Dan asked, chewing on a french fry. "I think they're pretty cool colors."

"That's because you didn't have to go out and buy a purple or gold dress," Caroline informed him. "You'll be wearing a tux."

"Our dresses don't *have* to be purple or gold," Robyn Schaffer spoke up. "That's just, like, a suggestion. The invitation says to wear 'bright jewel tones.'" She looked around at her girlfriends. "*My* dress is, like, this deep turquoise," she told them, lowering her voice as if sharing a major secret.

The other girls all nodded, making appreciative "mmmm" noises—which became startled shrieks as a sound like a gunshot tore through the cafeteria, followed immediately by dead silence.

Two hundred pairs of eyes swiveled toward the source of the noise. A short girl with glasses stood at the helium tank, holding the shredded remnants of a balloon in one hand. "Sorry," she squeaked.

The lunchroom activity resumed, noise level once again rising to normal.

Turning back to the table, Caroline muttered, "They should really be more careful. They can't afford to lose any more balloons—this place needs all the decorations it can get."

Michael snorted. "Please. There aren't enough decorations in the *world* to make this room look like anything but an ugly cafeteria." He pointed his Coke bottle toward the students unrolling the lines of crepe paper. "I say, if their main goal is for people to forget they're dancing in a lunchroom, they should just cut those streamers into blindfolds and make people put 'em on at the door."

Setting down his cheeseburger, Bennett Lee said, "Hmmm, guys. Sounds to me like the Redmonster's jealous."

Dan Futterman nodded at him. "It sure does."

Michael placed a hand on his chest. "Jealous? *Moi?*"

Bennett smiled smugly. "That's right—jealous. That *some* of us are going to the dance with our girlfriends and you aren't."

"Aren't going to the dance with your girlfriends?" Michael deadpanned.

Dan chucked a french fry at him. "You know what he means."

Michael picked up the fallen fry, wagging it in the air like a finger. "As a matter of fact, I *do* know. And you're absolutely right. In fact, I can picture it now: While you're both here, dressed up in your penguin suits, drinking Hawaiian Punch spiked with flat ginger ale and soaking up all the rich, romantic ambience that our puke green cafeteria has to offer, poor little ol' me will be stuck at home, crying my jealous eyes out while eating pizza and watching MTV. What a tragedy." He popped the french fry in his mouth.

Dan and Bennett shared a look. "Yup— *jealous*," they said in unison, and cracked up.

"And what about *you*, Caroline?" Pattye Grecko called over. "Why aren't *you* going to the dance? After all, you don't *have* to be asked by someone in order to attend."

"Yeah," Robyn cut in, "you can, like, go alone."

Caroline took a sip of iced tea. "Gee. Thanks for your concern, guys. You know, I *wanted* to go, but when I heard your boyfriends would be on the dance floor, I changed my mind. I value my toes too much."

Robyn and Pattye both rolled their eyes at Caroline. Just when it looked like they were about to retort, an announcement blared over the PA system.

"Attention. Will the following students please report to the principal's office: Michael Redmont, Caroline Knapp . . ."

"Ooh, sounds like somebody's in for it," Robyn Schaffer gloated.

". . . Cecily Vaughn, Mason Parker, Serena Waters, Robyn Schaffer . . ."

"It certainly does," Michael said to Robyn.

12:55 P.M.

About twenty students—all seniors—had been named over the loudspeaker. Once it was determined

96

that no one knew the reason for their mysterious summons, the murmuring group left the cafeteria and headed for the principal's office.

Along the way Caroline felt a tug on her elbow.

It was Michael. With a tilt of his head he indicated they should hold back. As the others moved on, he said, "You know, Knapsack, I was thinking—maybe you and I *should* go to the dance. Together."

Caroline's heart did a weird little flip-flop in her chest. "Seriously?" she croaked.

Michael's eyes lit up. "No—*un*seriously."

He must have noticed the look of confusion on her face because he quickly added, "Everyone here seems to think this dance is one of the most glamorous, important nights of the year." He nodded in front of them toward Robyn Schaffer and the others. "So I say, let's dress up as ridiculously as possible and then totally rag on everybody the whole night. Really show them all just how ludicrous they are. What do you say?"

Caroline didn't know what to say. But at least for the moment, she didn't have to worry about that.

They had just reached the principal's office.

1:06 P.M.

As it turned out, they weren't in trouble. However, once they found out the reason they *had* been called to the principal's office, Michael began to wonder if getting punished would have felt all that different.

"You think we have to wear these the rest of the day?" he whispered to Caroline.

He was talking about the large, satin sashes—the same kind worn by beauty-pageant contestants—that Principal Waxman had just draped over each of their shoulders. Both his and Caroline's ribbon read Funniest. Around the rest of the office other pairs of students sported similar ribbons, including ones for Most Athletic, Most Artistic, Most Musical, and Smartest.

"What I'd like to know," Caroline said, "is who voted on this. *I* sure didn't. Did you?"

"Yeah, right. Like I voted for *that*." Michael gestured toward Robyn Schaffer, who was in a Most-Popular sash.

Standing next to Michael, Serena Waters spun around, her eyes wide with concern. "You mean you guys *didn't vote?*" she cried. "There was a big ballot box outside the yearbook office! We posted flyers and made announcements and *everything!* Didn't your homeroom representative *tell* you?"

Caroline shook her head. "Um, I don't think so," she replied to the girl, whose sash read Most School Spirit.

"What's a homeroom representative?" Michael asked.

Serena rolled her eyes, but she was grinning.

Michael's own eyes swept the room, coming to rest on Mason Parker. Mason looked even more uncomfortable than Michael felt—which made sense, considering that he was wearing three times as many sashes. According to the huge satin ribbons, not only was Mason the Most-Popular guy in the twelfth grade; he also was the Most Athletic and one half of the Class Couple.

Michael searched for the second half.

He located Cecily Vaughn, in the matching sash, standing near Principal Waxman. She was frowning and looking at Mason.

Michael leaned over to Caroline. "What's up with Mason and Cecily?" he muttered under his breath.

"What do you mean?" she whispered back.

"I mean, for the class couple they certainly don't seem very coupleish, do they?" He paused, then added: "You think she's jealous that he has more ribbons than she does?"

Caroline screwed up her lips, considering the possibility. "That, or maybe she's upset there wasn't a category for Biggest Wardrobe."

Principal Waxman held up her hand. "All right, everybody," she announced. "Now that all of you have on your ribbons, we're going to head to the auditorium to take a group photo for the yearbook."

"But Mrs. Waxman," Cecily Vaughn complained, "none of us is dressed for photos! Can't we do it another day?"

Principal Waxman shook her head. "I'm afraid it's not up to me—it's up to the yearbook staff. You'd have to schedule it with their photographer. *And* arrange among yourselves to all get together again."

"*I* know!" Serena chirped. "There's going to be a yearbook photographer at the dance tonight. We can all get our picture taken then. Right, people?"

The other kids voiced their agreement. Then Robyn Schaffer spoke up. "Wait a minute, guys. I think some people here aren't going to *be* at the dance." She shot a pointed look in Caroline and Michael's direction.

"Not going? *Who's* not going?" Serena said, looking around in disbelief. "Whoever here's not going, raise your hand."

Michael started to raise his hand, but Caroline suddenly grabbed it, keeping it planted firmly down at his side. He turned to her, cocking an eyebrow.

She returned his gaze, giving his hand a squeeze. The look in her blue-gray eyes said: *Let's do it.*

Four

WHEN MICHAEL GOT home from school, his broken-down car—Suzie—wasn't in the driveway.

He panicked, thinking she'd been stolen—but then he noticed that the lights were on in the two-car garage. Peeking through the window, he saw Suzie parked inside, along with his grandfather, who was tinkering around in her engine.

Probably pushed her in there all by himself, the old fool.

A few minutes later Michael was inside as well, sitting behind the wheel of the Plymouth Valiant and telling his grandfather about his plans for the evening.

"Well, it's about time!" Gramps exclaimed before Michael was through. "I was wonderin' when you'd be followin' in my fancy footsteps." He craned his head out from behind the raised hood. "All right—give 'er a go."

Michael turned the key in the ignition. Nothing.

His grandfather backed away from the engine, scratching behind his ear with a wrench. "Course, you might not guess it, lookin' at me now, but I cut quite a rug in my day."

"Yeah, well, don't get your hopes up, Gramps. I don't think I'll be doing much dancing tonight."

His grandfather peered down at him, then disappeared behind the hood again. After a moment he called out, "Okay—try her now."

Michael turned the key . . . and Suzie purred to life.

Gramps slammed down the hood, smiling in satisfaction. Wiping his wrench off on a rag, he said, "So tell me, Mikey—who's the lucky girl?"

Michael cut the motor, climbing out of the car. "Her name's Caroline. And she's not the *lucky* girl—she's just a girl."

His grandfather tossed him an irritated look. "Any young lady dating a grandson of mine is lucky, my boy."

Michael said, "But that's just it. We're *not* dating. This isn't a date. We're just going to the dance together as a joke."

His grandfather's eyebrows shot up. "A joke?"

"Yeah. You know—to rag on the people who take it so seriously."

Gramps slipped the wrench back into his toolbox,

then closed the metal case with a loud bang. "All right. What's the matter with her?"

Michael laughed. "There's nothing the *matter* with her. It's just . . ." He hesitated, at a loss for words. "Well, if you met her, you'd know what I mean."

Gramps nodded, eyes narrowing. "I getcha. She's butt ugly."

"Oh—she's *definitely* not ugly," Michael responded, a little too loudly.

Gramps poked him on the chest. "Aha! So you think she's pretty."

Michael blinked, backing away. "What? I didn't say that."

"But it's true."

The air in the garage was beginning to feel warm. Michael shifted uncomfortably, taking a deep breath. "No, it's—I mean, *yes,* it's—I mean . . ."

He suddenly didn't know *what* he meant. Especially with his grandfather standing there, staring at him like that, looking all amused at his uneasiness.

Michael sighed in frustration. "I mean—*objectively*—sure. Like, if I were only just seeing Caroline for the first time, I would think she was pretty. But then she'd open her mouth and—"

"—and say something smart and funny, just like one of the guys," Gramps finished for him, eyes twinkling.

So the old man *did* understand. "Right," Michael answered, nodding vigorously. "Like one of the guys." He leaned back against Suzie and added, "Caroline's the kind of girl you like to hang with, not the kind you want to, *you* know . . ."

"Date?" his grandfather offered.

"Exactly."

Gramps stepped forward, putting his hands on Michael's shoulders. "Well, I think it's a cryin' shame, Mikey."

Michael frowned. "What is?"

"That you inherited all them good looks from me, when all any girl's ever gonna notice is that big ol' mouth of yours." He boxed his grandson lightly on the chin.

Michael laughed. "Well, gee, thanks for the good genes, Gramps. But to be honest, the only inheritance *I'm* interested in is hidden under that tarp." He nodded toward the other side of the garage, at the large vehicle hidden under its lambskin cover.

His grandfather looked over, then clucked his tongue. "Why, if you think you're gettin' the Duzer, my boy, you got another think comin'," he replied. "For your information, I plan to be *buried* in that car."

Michael clapped his grandfather on the shoulder. "Well, I hate to break it to you, Gramps. But if that's the case, then no one's gonna be at your funeral."

"Oh? And why's that, smart stuff?"

Michael grinned. "Because the day that car leaves this garage is the day the rest of this family drops dead from the shock."

★ ★ ★

"You simply can't *believe* how cold it was. *Tell* them how cold it was, Arthur."

Behind the wheel of the Lexus, Dr. Knapp said, "It was cold."

"It was *freezing*," Mrs. Knapp continued. "Freezing! I swear, they should post signs at the border. Big, red warning signs. Beware: This City Is Freezing. I thought I was going to *die*, it was so cold. Didn't you think I was going to die, Arthur?"

Dr. Knapp said, "I thought you were going to die."

Sitting beside Caroline in the backseat, Amy, Caroline's sister, laughed. "Well, gosh, Mom. What did you expect? Chicago *is* nicknamed the Windy City."

"Actually," Caroline elaborated, "I hear they originally wanted to nickname it the Oh-My-God-I-Feel-Like-I'm-Going-to-Die-It's-So-Cold-and-Windy City, but that was too long to fit on the souvenir mugs."

"Ooh—the souvenirs!" Mrs. Knapp exclaimed. "I almost forgot." She opened her large pocketbook and pulled out two crumpled shopping bags from inside, handing one to each of her daughters.

Caroline opened hers first, removing an extra-large printed T-shirt. "Gee, Mom," she said, smiling thinly, "you shouldn't have."

"Read what it says."

"I did."

"No—*out loud,*" her mother ordered. "Read it out loud so everyone can hear."

Caroline grimaced but obliged. "'My parents went on a trip to Chicago, and all I got was this lousy T-shirt.'"

Wow. How original.

In the passenger seat Mrs. Knapp cackled. "Isn't that a *riot?* I saw it in the hotel shop and said, 'This would be *perfect* for my Caroline, the little comedienne.' Isn't that shirt a riot, Arthur?"

Dr. Knapp said, "It's a riot."

"And how do *you* like *your* present, Amanda?" Mrs. Knapp called out in a singsongy voice.

Amy was holding a tiny Chicago Bulls jersey up to her chest. "Uh, gee, Mom. It's *nice* . . . but I think you may have underestimated my size a little."

Mrs. Knapp clucked her tongue. "It's not for *you,* dopey," she told her. "It's for the baby."

Amy grew pale. "Mother!" she exclaimed. "I can't believe you're giving me *baby gifts* when Jim and I won't even be *married* for another two weeks!"

"It's never too early to plan, sweetheart," Mrs. Knapp said.

Seeing the look of mortification on her sister's face, Caroline decided now would be a good time to change the subject. "Um . . . speaking of plans," she began, "Michael Redmont asked me to go with him to the winter dance to—"

Before she could finish saying "tonight," her mother and sister both let out enormous, high-pitched shrieks, very nearly causing Dr. Knapp to run the Lexus off the highway.

"Omigod!" Amy squealed, wrapping Caroline in an enormous hug. "Omigod! Omigod! Omigod!" She bounced Caroline up and down.

"Caroline!" her mother croaked, twisting around in her seat belt. "That's wonderful! Why didn't you tell us sooner?"

Caroline was still being bounced/smothered by Amy. "Er . . . it was kind of a spur-of-the-moment decision," she mumbled.

Amy abruptly released Caroline from her bear hug, now seizing her by the elbows. "So—who's this Michael Redmont? What does he look like? Is he cute?" Her voice was bubbling over with excitement.

"He's . . . a friend," Caroline replied, flustered by the question. She pictured Michael in her mind. "Kind of tall. Dark hair. Green eyes. I *guess* you could say he's cute. . . ."

"Omigod—you're *blushing!* Look, Mom, Caroline's *blushing!*"

"Of course she is," Mrs. Knapp said. "It's natural to blush when you're in love."

Caroline's jaw dropped. She stared back and forth between her mother and sister.

"I don't *believe* you two! I am *not* in *love!* Michael Redmont is just a friend of mine. He's not the man of my dreams!"

"Oh? And how do you know he's not the future son-in-law of *my* dreams?"

Caroline sighed in exasperation. "Aren't you

listening to me? Because we're *just friends*. We have no romantic interest in each other whatsoever. Honest."

"You never know, Caroline," Mrs. Knapp told her, shaking a finger. "I mean, who'd have thought that the fat, shy, redheaded boy who asked my Amanda to *her* first dance would someday be asking for her hand in marriage?"

"Jim is not fat!" Amy screeched at the back of her mother's head. "He's *big boned.*"

"Big boned, big boned," Mrs. Knapp conceded, rolling her eyes. She glanced down at her watch. "Well, thank *God* we're headed to the mall, Caroline. We can get you a nice dress and some shoes and do *something* about that hair. . . ."

"I don't need a dress."

"Of course you need a dress," Mrs. Knapp went on. "What are you going to wear? A bedsheet?"

Caroline laughed. "Hey—that's not a bad idea."

Mrs. Knapp turned to stare at her daughter, a glimmer of worry creeping into her eyes. "I hope you're joking."

"No, I'm not joking," Caroline answered. "Michael and I are both going in gag outfits."

"Gag outfits?" Amy said, confused. "What do you mean? Is it a costume dance?"

Caroline shook her head. "No, it's a regular, real formal. Michael and I will be the only ones not properly dressed for it."

"The only ones . . . ," Mrs. Knapp repeated, her voice sounding hollow.

Caroline nodded. "Uh-huh. We're going to dress up in really ridiculous clothes to show everyone else how silly they all are. It'll be hilarious."

"Hilarious . . . ," Amy said blankly, sliding away from her sister.

It was suddenly very quiet inside the Lexus.

After a tense moment Mrs. Knapp said, "Well, I've never heard of going to a formal dance as a joke. Never in all my life." She turned to her husband. "Arthur, did you ever hear of such a thing in all your—"

Dr. Knapp said, "Never in all my life."

Five

4:47 *P.M.*

MICHAEL HATED THE mall at Christmastime. Hated it. In fact, given the choice between shopping at the Riverside Mall in December or skinny dipping in a lake full of piranhas, he'd seriously consider taking his chances with the fish.

First, there was the small matter of *parking*. No need to elaborate on that one.

Then the constant, inescapable barrage of piped-in holiday music. Nauseating. Michael had a special hatred for "The Christmas Song," by Nat King Cole. It was bad enough that this particular song seemed to come on every five minutes. But what made it truly unbearable was that when Michael was little, he'd made the mistake of naming his pet guinea pig Chestnut. Since then every time he heard Nat King Cole sing, *"Chestnuts roasting on an open fire,"* the vision *he'd* get (instead of sugarplums dancing) was of a beloved family pet being charbroiled.

And finally, there was the shopping itself. No matter how well one prepared, it invariably turned into a test of nerves. Take this afternoon, for instance. Even though he'd known exactly what he wanted and where to find it, he'd still ended up waiting in a crowded checkout line for over twenty minutes.

Change stashed away and bag in hand, Michael heard a familiar voice suddenly call out his name. He spun to see the Rat pushing toward him through the busy corridor, trailed closely by Ira Berg, lead singer of Xenophobic Linguistics. Both boys carried black garment bags over their shoulders.

"Hey, Redmonster," the Rat said, pulling up alongside him. "You here to visit Santa?" He pointed toward the slew of parents and children who were lined up a few yards away.

Michael snorted, and the three boys started moving toward the exit. Michael nodded at the garment bags. "Those what I think they are?"

"Yep," said Ira. "Our penguin suits."

"I tell ya, Mikey," the Rat muttered, "I'm beginning to think you have the right idea by staying home tonight. These rental tuxes cost a fortune."

"Actually, I decided to go," Michael told them.

"Get out of here!" the Rat exclaimed. "Seriously?"

Michael stopped walking. "Can you guys keep a secret?" he asked. Opening his shopping bag, Michael took out his purchase and held it up to his chest.

It was a simple, black cotton T-shirt, but one side was printed to look like the front of a tuxedo jacket, complete with bow tie and white ruffle. It even had a cartoonish red carnation drawn on the fake lapel.

Ira Berg let out a guffaw. "Excellent, dude!"

"Wow," the Rat said. "I remember seeing that shirt when I was a kid. I can't believe they still make it."

"You kidding?" Michael responded. "My friend, you are looking at a truly timeless classic in the rich and varied history of novelty T-shirts." He displayed the garment proudly. "Without a doubt, the Poor-Man's Tuxedo ranks right up there with the equally famous I'm with Stupid shirt."

Ira stared at him. "You're actually planning to wear that to the dance?"

Michael nodded. "Yup. Me and Caroline Knapp are both going in gag outfits. But you can't tell anyone," he added quickly.

"So what's Knapsack gonna wear?" Ira asked.

"I don't know yet," Michael answered. "But if I know Caroline, I'm sure she'll whip up some kind of crazy dress."

The Rat chuckled knowingly. "I have a hard enough time picturing what she'd look like in a *regular* dress."

"*I* don't . . . ," Ira said, stopping dead in his tracks. He was staring across the busy corridor with a strange expression on his face.

Michael followed his gaze toward the outside of Lara Ling Designs, one of the mall's more upscale boutiques. The large storefront window had been decorated with a whirlwind of delicate silver snowflakes, but it was what was visible *through* the sparkling windowpane that suddenly took Michael's breath away.

I don't believe it. . . .

"Bro," the Rat whispered. "Is that *Knapsack?*"

Caroline Knapp was standing atop a small platform inside the boutique, in the center of a pool of golden light.

She had on the most amazing dress Michael had ever seen.

The sleeveless, off-the-shoulder gown looked like something a princess should wear. Or maybe a movie star.

"Wow," the Rat commented, "she sure cleans up good."

Michael could only stare and nod dumbly.

He couldn't believe that the elegant creature framed in the window before him was the same person he'd sat next to at lunch that afternoon. The same person he'd nearly mauled to death in the backseat of the Rat's car that morning. The same person he'd known for the past two years and never once imagined, beneath all the baggy sweatshirts and sweaters, could actually be so . . . so . . . *different.*

It was as if someone had suddenly flipped the page on Michael's mental picture of Caroline, and now her head was resting on top of a completely unfamiliar body—and yet a body that undeniably fit. And fit flawlessly.

In the dress shop Caroline raised her hands up over her head, assuming the classic position of someone being held at gunpoint. Instead of a robber a small, dark-haired woman appeared, circling nimbly around the platform. Every few seconds her tiny, birdlike hands would dart forward.

"Uh . . . Mikey?" the Rat asked, nudging his arm.

Michael shook his head and blinked, as if coming out of a trance. "Huh?"

"When you and Caroline discussed going to the dance, are you *sure* you mentioned the part about wearing the gag outfits?"

Michael looked at the Rat, annoyed. "Of course I'm sure. That's the whole id—" He suddenly interrupted himself, eyes darting back toward the boutique window. "Oh—you don't think—you don't think she's getting that dress for *tonight*. . . ."

The Rat crossed his arms. "How else do you explain it?"

"She's probably just, you know, shopping. . . ."

"Yeah, *riiight*." The Rat smirked. "She just *happens* to be shopping for a *purple* dress on the night of the winter formal."

"You gotta admit, that would be quite a coincidence," Ira cut in.

Michael's heart began to race. "I swear, guys. I told her we were going as a joke. I *swear*. . . ."

"Looks like the joke's on you, Mikey," the Rat said. "Apparently Knapsack thought you were asking her out for real."

Michael suddenly felt sick. As if the mall were closing in around him, suffocating him. "How could she have misunderstood me?" he mumbled. His voice sounded weak. He could barely hear it above the blaring music and thunderous crowd noise pressing on his eardrums.

"Hey—don't sweat it too much, bro," Ira said. "You're a lucky dog. Who knew Knapp had such major babe potential?"

"Yeah, Redmonster. It's no big deal," the Rat agreed. He turned away from Michael, gesturing toward Caroline. "So, you and Knapsack got your wires crossed. So what? If you're worried that the truth will hurt her feelings, all you gotta do is go rent yourself a real tux, and she'll never know you weren't really serious. No harm, no foul. Am I right?"

By the time the Rat turned around for the response, Michael had already disappeared.

4:53 P.M.

"Say, Caroline . . . do you know those boys?"

Mrs. Knapp was staring behind Caroline out of the boutique's floor-to-ceiling window.

"What boys? Where?" Perched atop the fitting platform, Caroline attempted to follow her mother's gaze—but was instantly rewarded with a sharp jab in the small of her back.

"Hold still," the tiny seamstress ordered, somehow making her words intelligible even though she had a dozen or so straight pins clenched tightly in her lips. "I'm almost through."

Yeah, Caroline thought sorely. *Through to my spinal column.*

"You know, Amy," she called over to her sister, "if I'd known being a bridesmaid was going to involve this much bloodshed, I would've told you no."

Amy was behind a dressing screen, changing out of her wedding dress. She stepped from behind the divider, buttoning up her sweater. "And if *I'd* known you'd be giving me so much grief, I wouldn't have—*oh, Caroline!*" she gushed as her eyes fell upon her sister. "You look *so . . . so . . .*"

"Purple?" Caroline suggested.

"*Beautiful!* Doesn't she, Mom?"

"Of course she does." Mrs. Knapp lowered her copy of *Modern Bride,* rising from her seat and crossing to Amy's side. *"Both* my daughters are beautiful. Sometimes I wonder to myself, What in the world could I have done to wind up with two such lovely girls?"

Amy laughed. "So—how does it feel, Caroline?"

"How does what feel?"

"The dress. How does the *dress* feel?"

"Oh." Caroline placed her hands on her hips and did a couple of perfunctory trunk twists. "It seems to fit okay," she said, then paused, knitting her brow. "But I don't think I can take a deep breath." The formfitting velvet bodice flowed into a floor-length, shimmering violet satin skirt.

"You're not *supposed* to be able to take a deep breath—you're supposed to look beautiful!" Amy pointed out.

"But not *too* beautiful," Mrs. Knapp cut in, slipping an arm around her older daughter's shoulders.

"I won't have you attracting all the attention away from my Amanda on her wedding day."

Looking down at them, Caroline felt her mouth curl into a half smile. "Oh, I wouldn't worry about that, Mom. Believe me, in this dress the only attention I'll be attracting is from the fashion police."

Amy's face instantly fell. "What's the matter? Don't you like the dress?"

Oops. There I go. Sticking my foot in my mouth again . . .

"No, it's not that—I like the dress. I love it," Caroline added hastily. "I mean, the style is fine. It's just—you know—the *color.* . . ."

"What's wrong with the *color?*" Amy shrieked.

. . . and shoving it in even further.

Caroline took an uncomfortable breath. "Uh, there's nothing *wrong* with it, exactly. It's just that, well . . . I'm just not used to seeing this particular shade of purple . . . except on a singing and dancing dinosaur."

"Ohh, don't you pay any attention to her, Amy, darling," Mrs. Knapp said, pecking her older daughter on the cheek. "No matter what Caroline says, this is *your* wedding, which means *you* get to choose the colors that *you* want. When it's Caroline's turn up at the altar, *she* can have whatever colors *she* wants." Mrs. Knapp shot Caroline a withering glance. "Although I'm not quite sure they *make* bridesmaid dresses in sweatshirt gray."

Caroline put a hand on her stomach, teetering on the platform. "Don't make me laugh, Mom. I'll burst a seam."

Six

5:01 P.M.

"*CHESTNUTS ROASTING ON an open fire* . . ."
Nat King Cole's vibrato-rich voice crooned loudly as Michael pushed his way through the entrance of One Night Affair. He was breathing hard, having run the entire length of the mall and up two escalators on his way to the tuxedo-rental shop.

Behind the counter was a plump woman in a Santa cap. "Let me guess," she said, sizing him up through her red, rhinestone-rimmed glasses. "The dance at Riverside High. Am I right?"

Michael merely nodded, still too out of breath to respond.

"I knew it." The saleslady licked her finger, flipping a page in a large, black ledger. "What's your name?" she asked, removing a pen from behind her ear.

"Redmont," he replied, feeling his heartbeat slow back down to normal. "Michael Redmont."

The saleslady's eyes scanned the list of names written down in the book. "Redmont . . . Redmont . . ." After a second she looked up, frowning. "I'm sorry. I don't seem to have a Redmont listed here."

"Oh," Michael said, "that's because I, uh, didn't order a tux yet—I mean, I still need to. Order one. For tonight." He smiled at her weakly. "If it's not a problem."

The saleslady's frown deepened. "It *could* be a problem," she told him, tapping her pen on the countertop. "Do you know your jacket size?"

Michael's heartbeat started accelerating again. "Uh . . . forty long?" he told her.

The saleslady stared at him grimly. "It's a problem."

"Forty regular?"

"Honey," the saleslady said, slamming the ledger closed. "I don't know what they're feeding you kids at that high school, but I got a hundred and sixty-eight tuxes rented out tonight, all to Riverside boys, and I'd say a good hundred of them are size forties. We had to order in extras from the warehouse." She tucked the pen back behind her ear.

"You mean you're *all out?*" Michael asked, his voice becoming a desperate squeak.

The woman's expression softened a bit. "I didn't say that," she replied. "Let me see what I can do here." Turning around, she headed into a back room, singing along with Nat King Cole, *"He's loading lots of toys and goodies on his sleigh. . . ."*

After a moment she returned. She was smiling, holding up a black garment bag in her pudgy pink hand. Michael sighed heavily, relieved—and a little surprised to realize he'd been holding his breath the whole time she'd been away.

"It's your lucky day," she announced, hanging the garment bag on a clothes hook between two mirrors. "This is the very last one we have in your size."

Oh, thank you, God. Thank you, thank you, thank you.

The saleslady unzipped the protective cover with a loud flourish—*zzzzzzzzt!*—then carefully peeled back the black vinyl flaps so that Michael could get a good look.

And a good look he got. Perhaps *too* good. For the next fifteen seconds he stared at the tuxedo hanging in front of him . . . and found himself wondering just how, exactly, they defined the term "lucky day" on the planet this woman called home.

The tux was yellow. *Yellow.*

And not just *any* yellow. *School-bus* yellow. School-bus yellow with darker, mustard yellow lapels and pocket flaps, all outlined in braided, black satin trim.

"We call it the El Dorado." The saleslady waved her hands up and down the jacket the same way a spokesmodel on a TV game show might show off a new dishwasher.

With a feeling like indigestion, Michael noticed that the saleslady was waiting for some kind of response. He swallowed hard.

"The, um, *lapels* . . . ," he stammered. "They're, uh—"

"Velveteen," she cut in, smiling wider. "*Very* snazzy."

Actually, hideous *is the word I was thinking.*

Michael smiled back at her uncomfortably. "Gee, I don't know. . . ."

The saleslady's smile faltered. "What's not to know? Look—" With one swift motion she snatched the tuxedo off the wall, smacked it up against Michael's chest, and spun him around toward the mirror. "Do you see what I mean? Eh? *Ehhh?*"

Sure, Michael was tempted to respond, *if you mean, see the big loser in the ugly yellow tux.*

Instead he just stared at his reflection. It wasn't easy. The top of the hanger was jammed up beneath his nose, looking like a curving metal mustache. The tuxedo itself dangled below his chin like a long, yellow bib.

Not surprisingly, seeing the mirror image of the tux did little to change Michael's mind as to how absolutely nauseating it was. On the contrary— now he had the added bonus of seeing how really awful his face looked on top of it.

Yup, he thought, taking it all in, *if there's ever been any doubt, now it's official: Yellow is not my color.*

The saleslady's voice interrupted his thoughts. "I'm telling you," she gushed in his ear. "This tux is *you.*"

Opening his eyes, Michael was suddenly seized

with the overwhelming urge to laugh. The saleslady was absolutely right. The tux *was* him. In fact, twenty minutes ago the El Dorado would have been just what he was looking for: an outfit that was perfectly, hideously wrong for a formal affair. It practically made the T-shirt in his shopping bag seem like the more conservative choice of attire.

But now his priorities had changed. Now the mental picture of himself in the yellow tux, standing beside Caroline in her beautiful violet dress, made him want to throw up.

"Thanks anyway," he told her, pushing the hanger away from his chest and sprinting out the door.

6:09 P.M.

Caroline had a tough decision to make. And she had to make it soon. She was so caught up in solving her dilemma that she was barely aware of the knock on her bedroom door or of her own voice calling out, "Come in."

The door opened and Amy entered, carrying the newly altered bridesmaid gown on its padded hanger. "You left this downstairs," she said, crossing to Caroline's closet and hanging the violet dress inside.

Caroline swiveled around in her desk chair. "Amy—*you* help me decide." She held up two items for her sister to see. "Pink fuzzy dice or pine-tree-shaped air fresheners?"

Amy put her hands on her hips, looking confused. "And just what exactly am I supposed to be deciding here? The better stocking stuffer for Dad?"

Caroline laughed. "No, silly. Which do you think I should wear for earrings tonight?" She spun back around in her chair, holding both choices up to her earlobes. "I can't make up my mind," she said, frowning at herself in the mirror. "At first I was leaning toward the fuzzy dice since they're the absolute all-time symbols of bad taste . . . but the pine trees have been growing on me. For one thing, they're much more seasonal. And considering that the dance is being held in the cafeteria, they come with the added bonus of being able to mask foul odors—*definitely* a plus. What do you think?"

Amy stared Caroline's reflection in the eye. "I think my kid sister has lost her mind, that's what I think."

"*Exactly* the reaction I'm going for," Caroline said, "but it doesn't answer the question."

Amy sighed. "The trees will probably be more comfortable."

Caroline nodded. "Thanks, Ames. I knew I could count on you."

"Don't mention it." Amy was about to leave when she noticed the other items resting on Caroline's desktop. "Hey—are those my new curlers?"

"Yeah," Caroline replied. "Will you help me pin up my hair?"

"Well, gee," Amy said sarcastically, crossing to her younger sister's chair. "I suppose it wouldn't be very sisterly of me to say no, especially after I was good enough to lend them to you in the first place."

Caroline hunched her shoulders guiltily. "Sorry," she apologized. "I guess I should've asked. But I just figured you'd say okay . . . seeing as it *is* my big night and all." She dragged the toe of her shoe back and forth across the carpet. "Don't you want me to look *purty?*"

Amy shot her sister an irritated look, but it was only for show. Picking up Caroline's brush, she dutifully began separating out a section of her younger sister's long, light brown hair. "You know, Caroline," she said, scooping up one of the large, neon pink plastic spools, "if you really want to wear your hair curly for tonight, you should use my curling iron. There's not much time for these to set."

"Oh, I don't want curly hair," Caroline explained. "I want to leave the curlers *in.*"

Amy paused halfway through rolling up the strand of hair. "I should have known." Shaking her head wearily, she continued winding up the roller, bobby-pinned it in place, and moved on to the next section of hair. She worked quickly and diligently, and soon Caroline's head wore a virtual helmet of pink plastic.

"Mom's right, you know, Caroline," Amy said when she was nearly finished.

"About what?"

"About how you never can tell whether someone is just a friend or whether they're about to become more."

"Oh, *please*." Caroline huffed. "You don't still think Michael and I are actually—"

"No, no, no," Amy interrupted, holding up a hand in surrender. "I know you two are just going as a joke. I just wanted to point out that this *can,* for *some* people, turn out to be a very special night."

"Yeah, yeah, I've heard the story," Caroline said. "Once upon a time, Jim asked you to the holiday dance, and even though you didn't really want to go with him, you said yes, and then when you were on the dance floor, he kissed you, and suddenly there were skyrockets going off and violins playing and birds singing and you were madly in love. The end."

"Oh, that's not what happened at all," Amy said. "I mean, I *did* fall in love with Jim that night, but it had nothing to do with him kissing me. And there *weren't* any fireworks or violins playing or anything like what they say is supposed to happen in books and movies." She tilted her head slightly. "In fact, it was just the opposite. It was at that dance, for the first time, that all these small, subtle things about our friendship—things I'd never really noticed or thought about much—suddenly took on a whole new significance for me."

"Like what?" Caroline asked—and immediately wished she hadn't.

But it was too late to take it back. Amy's eyes were already glazing over with the far-off, sickeningly blissful expression that appeared whenever she spoke about her fiancé.

"Oh, *you* know . . . ," Amy said dreamily, "like

how whenever Jim and I would run into each other in the hall or someplace, we'd always share this kind of intense, private smile, as if there was some amazing joke that only he and I knew about. Or the way when I'd be sitting next to him and our knees or hands or elbows would touch by accident, he wouldn't flinch and pull away, not even a little. Or how we could always finish each other's sentences, as if we were reading each other's—"

"Just a second," Caroline interrupted. "I believe this is the part where I'm supposed to barf."

"Oh, ha, ha, ha," Amy said, rolling up the final section of Caroline's hair. "All I'm saying is, you can make fun of the bad dancing and the gaudy dresses and the cheesy decorations all you want, but don't knock falling in love. It *has* been known to happen, you know. Even in stinky cafeterias."

"This message brought to you by the folks at Hallmark," Caroline announced, holding up her hairbrush like a microphone.

Amy sighed in exasperation. "And you better not lose any of these curlers," she said, bobby pinning the last hair roller in place with an extra-vicious jab. "I'm gonna need them for the wedding."

Seven

6:19 P.M.

C'*MON, C'MON* . . . STANDING in the kitchen with the phone pressed against his ear, Michael sighed heavily. *Answer already.*

He crossed to the kitchen table, set down the huge business directory he was holding, and took a seat. Again. It seemed like he'd walked the short distance from the wall phone to the table a hundred times over the past twenty minutes. Picking up his pencil, he did an actual tally.

There were thirteen pencil lines scribbled through thirteen phone numbers in the section Formal Wear—Rental & Sales of the thick yellow book lying open before him. That meant he'd made thirteen trips to the phone, dialed thirteen phone numbers, and placed thirteen futile calls in the pathetic attempt to track down a tuxedo—all ending in either a recorded voice informing him that a particular rental office was closed for the evening or a live voice informing him that he should have called much, much earlier.

Now, after nearly a dozen rings and still no answer at this latest number, Michael started making his fourteenth scribble of the night.

"Happy holidays from Tuxedo Junction," a young woman's voice bubbled out of the earpiece, startling him.

"Uh—yes," Michael fumbled. "I'm calling about renting a—"

"Ho, ho, hold, please," the voice interrupted. There was a click, and suddenly Nat King Cole was singing in his ear: *"Chestnuts roasting on an open fire . . ."*

The pencil in Michael's hand snapped in two.

Sitting across the table from him, Gramps looked up from his project of the evening: a pile of metal disks, gears, and springs that might or might not have been an alarm clock in a past life. The old man opened his mouth, looking like he was about to make one of his usual wry comments, but Michael glared at him, and he snapped his mouth shut fast. Setting down his screwdriver and pliers, Gramps pushed his chair away from the table, got up, and quietly headed out of the kitchen.

Michael watched his grandfather leave, suddenly feeling guilty. After all, it wasn't the old guy's fault that Michael was such a major screwup. He was about to call after him to apologize when there was another click on the line and the bubbly voice was back. "Thanks for holding. Can I help you?"

"Would it be possible for me to rent a tuxedo for tonight?" he asked, bracing himself for the answer. "Black, size forty long?"

"Yup."

"You're *sure* you have a size-*forty-long* tuxedo that I can rent from you *tonight? A black* tuxedo?"

"I'm sure."

"Great!" Michael said, leaping up. "My last name is Redmont. Please hold it for me, and I'll be down there in about half an hour."

"Oh—that'll be too late," the bubbly voice said. "We're closing in ten minutes."

Michael slammed the receiver down in its cradle.

Then he began banging his forehead against the wall. *What*—bang!—*did I do*—bang!—*to deserve this?*—bang! bang! bang!

He groaned. The thought of phoning another tux shop made his stomach turn.

Besides, what was the point? He already knew what the result would be. He could feel it deep in his bones: cruel, soul-crushing disappointment.

For some reason—for some horrible, inexplicable reason—the entire universe seemed to be working against him tonight. It was as if cosmic forces had aligned for the express purpose of keeping him from getting his hands on a tuxedo.

He took a deep breath, straightening up. No, right now there was only one course of action that made any sense. Only one call to make, and it *wasn't* to another tux shop.

He dialed without even knowing what he was going to say.

"Hello?" a man answered.

"Uh, hello . . . Mr. Knapp?"

"*Doctor* Knapp," the voice corrected.

Michael winced. *Oops.* "Dr. Knapp. Uh, this is Michael Redmont. May I please speak to Caroline?"

"Just a moment."

Michael heard Dr. Knapp place down the phone, then call out to his daughter. After a few seconds Caroline picked up on another extension.

"Hello?"

Michael swallowed hard. "Hey, Knapsack. It's me, Michael."

"What's up, Redmonster?"

He could just imagine her, standing there at her phone, probably in her dress. That beautiful, beautiful *dress* . . .

Michael's knees felt weak. He turned around, bracing his shoulders against the kitchen wall for support.

Go ahead, Mikey. Say it: You gotta cancel on her tonight because you're a big, fat, size-forty-long loser.

"Um, I know this is horrible of me, and I'll totally understand if you hate me for it with a deep, consuming kind of hatred, but I'm afraid that I'm going to have to—"

The words died in his throat as Gramps came back into the kitchen, smiling mysteriously and holding . . . a *black tuxedo.*

Michael's jaw dropped open. He stared at his grandfather in astonishment.

"Going to have to what?" Caroline asked. "Redmonster? You there?"

"Going to have to pick you up a little later than planned," he replied in a heated rush. "Say, um, seven thirty-five?"

"Gee," Caroline said. "A whopping five-minute difference. I can feel the deep, consuming hatred bubbling up in me already. See you then."

"Bye." Michael absently hung up the phone and turned to his grandfather. "Where'd you *get* that?" he asked, pointing in amazement.

"Hmmm . . . Paris, I think," Gramps said, scratching his chin. "Or maybe it was London."

Michael was speechless. "But—But—"

His grandfather's green eyes sparkled. "Actually, it was your grandma who got it for me. Picked it out on our honeymoon," he explained. "I'd married her in my army uniform, you see, but she said a groom just wasn't a groom without a top hat and tails." He smiled at the memory.

He held out the suit to Michael. "I think you and me are about the same size," he added, giving his grandson a wink.

Michael stepped forward, taking the tuxedo from his grandfather.

One thing became instantly apparent: His grandmother had had good taste. The expertly tailored, fine-wool jacket had glossy, black satin lapels and an ivory-colored satin lining. Michael spun the hanger around. Sure enough, the back of the jacket extended down into two long, tapered tails. It was the kind of tuxedo a famous orchestra conductor might wear. Or maybe a prince.

In other words, in the wide world of formal wear, his grandfather's tux was the archenemy of the El Dorado.

7:32 P.M.

"How do I look?"

Placing her hands on her hips, Caroline assumed the bland, expressionless gaze of a runway model, strutting across her room on an imaginary catwalk. She strolled with remarkable grace, considering the fact that she was wearing her father's clunky rubber snow boots and had a yellow vinyl tablecloth pinned around her waist for a skirt. Reaching the door, she spun around sharply. Her air-freshener earrings swayed like two tree-shaped pendulums above the brown paper grocery sack she'd formed into a blouse.

Amy was sitting on the bed, watching her sister's one-woman fashion show with a vaguely constipated look on her face. *"There's* a look you won't find in the pages of *Vogue,"* she said.

Caroline laughed, then took a seat at her desk. Leaning forward, she peered into the light-up makeup mirror that was set on top. "Are you sure these things will stay on?" she asked, tugging gently at her inhumanly long eyelashes.

"Not if you keep doing that, they won't."

Sitting up straight, Caroline practiced opening and closing her eyes a couple of times. "I feel like I could catch flies with these things."

"I wouldn't worry," Amy told her. "It's a proven fact that metallic blue eye shadow frightens away the majority of earth's species—including all eligible bachelors."

The doorbell rang.

"Speaking of eligible bachelors . . . ," Amy said, glancing at her watch, "this one's right on time."

Despite herself Caroline felt her pulse race. "Oh, jeez," she said. "I haven't finished my makeup. Could you go down and get him while I finish up?"

Amy was already heading out the door.

"Go quick," Caroline called after her, "before Mom gets there!"

Turning back to the makeup mirror, Caroline rooted around in her makeup bag, selecting her most garish shade of lipstick: a bright, candy-apple red she hadn't played with since she was twelve. She applied an even coat to her bottom lip, then carefully traced the delicate M-shaped curve of the upper one. Recapping the tube, she admired the result in the mirror. It was a perfect application. Not a single smudge or—

Wait a minute. What was I thinking?

She could hardly imagine what kind of outrageous costume the Redmonster was wearing downstairs. But whatever he had on, she wasn't *about* to let him outweigh her on the tackiness scale.

Uncapping the lipstick again, Caroline haphazardly smeared an uneven, half-inch line of red around the entire perimeter of her mouth, then smacked her lips together and blew a kiss at her reflection.

There. That's *more like it.*

Feeling inspired, Caroline rummaged around in the makeup bag again. Holding a black eyeliner pencil, she drew a heart-shaped beauty mark on her right cheek.

Better, much better. But it still needs something.

"Hmmm . . ." Caroline pressed her clown lips together, thinking hard. *What can it be?* Then, eyes crinkling in glee, she knew what was missing—or rather, what *wasn't* missing. Plucking a tissue from the dispenser on her desk, she smiled widely and had started blackening in one of her incisors when she heard footsteps approaching in the hall. The door creaked open behind her.

"Uh, Caroline . . . ?" Amy whispered.

"Yay-ess?" she replied, leaning far back in her chair and rapidly batting her fake eyelashes.

When Caroline saw the pale, stricken look on her sister's face, she sat up straight, her gap-toothed grin fading. "What is it? Where's Michael?"

Instead of answering, Amy just motioned with her finger, beckoning Caroline out into the hall.

Caroline followed her sister, who stopped at the end of the hallway, just around the corner from where the stairwell led down to the foyer below.

"Shhh." Amy held up a warning hand, keeping Caroline back, then peered furtively around the wall like a spy.

"What's wrong?" Caroline hissed, not sure why they were whispering.

Amy ignored her. After a second she backed away, indicating that Caroline should now step forward and take a look. Annoyed but curious, Caroline peeked her head around the corner—

—and nearly choked on the huge lump that suddenly lodged in her throat.

Michael Redmont was standing near the foot of the stairs, dressed in the most elegant tuxedo she had ever seen. It was the old-fashioned kind of tux—the kind with tails—but on Michael it looked absolutely charming. Even though he was facing away from her, she could see that the crisp black suit fit as if it had been expressly tailored for him. He looked stunningly handsome, if a little uncomfortable, rocking back and forth on his heels, waiting.

Waiting for *her,* she realized, feeling her heart skip a beat.

Down below, Michael took a deep, adorably nervous breath, shifting something from one hand to the other in order to check his wristwatch. With a pang of sweet surprise Caroline saw that it was a clear-plastic corsage box. The flower inside was white with violet accents. An orchid, perhaps, although it might also be a—

Never mind, you stupid twit! Caroline's thoughts screamed in her brain. *He was serious! He*

*was completely, utterly serious about tonight, and
the whole time you thought he was joking!*

Then, suddenly remembering how she was
dressed, she gasped in horror.

Below, Michael reacted at the sound, turning in
her direction. Caroline quickly pulled her head out
of sight, then pressed her back firmly against the
wall, squeezing her eyes closed.

The whole world suddenly felt off balance. Either
gravity itself had somehow been increased, or someone had just filled her stomach with about fifty
pounds of wet cement. She started to slide down the
wall—helplessly, hopelessly—then felt Amy seize her
by the elbow, jerk her to her feet, and drag her
quickly back down the hall toward her bedroom.

Once inside the room Amy slammed the door
closed and leaned up against it heavily, as if holding
back an angry mob. *"I thought you said he was
going in a gag outfit!"* she whispered shrilly.

Caroline sat on her bed in a daze. "That's what I
thought," she whispered back. "Oh God, oh God . . ."
She collapsed backward onto the mattress, only to be
painfully reminded of the huge plastic curlers still
rolled in her hair. She immediately sprang up again,
clutching her head in panic. *"What am I gonna do?"*

Amy eyed her younger sister steadily, saying
nothing for what seemed like forever. Then—as if
arriving at a decision—she nodded once to herself
and leaped into action. Crossing purposefully over
to the desk, she grabbed the tissue box, tossing it on
the bed. "The first thing you're going to do is wipe

off that makeup," she ordered, already moving to the closet. "Then you're going to take those ridiculous curlers out of your hair and change into a *real* dress."

"What real dress?" Caroline said dismally. "I don't have any—" She stopped herself midsentence, seeing what her sister was removing from the clothes rack. "Oh, Amy, you don't mean—"

Her sister nodded solemnly. "Oh yes, I *do* mean," she replied, lying the violet bridesmaid dress down on the bed next to the tissue box.

"But—"

"But nothing," Amy continued, placing her hands on her hips. "You either wear this dress, Caroline, or I go downstairs right now and tell that poor, deluded, absolutely *gorgeous* young man what a horrible, horrible mistake he made asking my moronic kid sister to a formal."

Caroline took a deep breath, then nodded, resigned. "Okay." She began pulling tissues out of the box, wiping off her mouth. "Okay."

Amy frowned at her. "Looks like you're gonna hafta use cold cream," she said, crossing back toward the door. "In the meantime I'd better go protect Michael from the parental menace." She opened the door.

"Wait!" Caroline stood up in alarm. "What are you going to tell him?"

Amy turned, one hand on the knob. "I'm just going to tell him the truth."

"What?"

"That you're still busy getting dressed, silly," Amy clarified. Then she winked. "Relax, sis. We girls are *never* supposed to be ready on time. He won't know anything's wrong. Trust me."

She stepped out into the hall, then poked her head back in.

"But hurry," she added, "before Mom sinks in her claws and scares him away."

Eight

7:54 P.M.

"AND *THIS* IS a sonogram showing Caroline during the twelfth week of pregnancy."

Mrs. Knapp pointed to yet another photo in the massive album she'd spread open on Michael's lap. "Isn't she cute?" she continued, tracing a portion of the blurry, black-and-white image with her fingernail. "*There's* her little head, and *there's* her little spine. See?"

Michael didn't see, but he nodded all the same. "Oh yeah. Her little spine. How 'bout that?" He smiled his millionth smile of the evening, certain that at any moment the muscles in his face were going to snap and break like overstretched rubber bands.

Mrs. Knapp leaned toward him across the couch, lowering her voice. "I know what you're wondering about this *next* sonogram, Michael, and the answer is *yes:* Caroline *does* have a little tail. But *all* babies do at that stage. Isn't that right, Arthur?"

Sitting across the room in an easy chair, Dr. Knapp said, "All babies have tails."

"My husband's an obstetrician," Mrs. Knapp said. She put her hand on Michael's arm, her eyes glinting keenly. "And which branch of medicine did you say *you* wanted to study again, Michael?"

Michael shifted uncomfortably. *Uh, the one where you learn acting?*

"I . . . didn't say," he answered.

"That's perfectly all right," Mrs. Knapp said, patting his shoulder and pulling the photo album onto her lap. "You'll have plenty of time to decide at med school. Isn't that right, Arthur?"

Dr. Knapp said, "Plenty of time."

Speaking of time, Michael wondered, *where is Caroline?* Her sister had said she was running a little late, but that was ages ago. He must've been sitting on this sofa, looking at photos with Mrs. Knapp, for at least an hour since then. Maybe longer.

Mrs. Knapp nudged his arm. "Your cocoa's getting cold." She nodded toward the coffee table, where a ceramic mug was resting. The words *World's Best Son-in-law* were printed on its side.

"Oh—thanks," Michael said, reaching forward and taking a huge sip. Setting the cup back down, he managed to sneak a peek at his wristwatch.

Seven fifty-five. He'd been there just twenty minutes. It only *felt* like hours.

He'd give Caroline five more minutes.

Taking a deep breath, he leaned back on the couch, and Mrs. Knapp slid the heavy photo album on his lap once again, pinning him in his seat. She flipped another page.

"Ooh! Now in *this* sonogram you can actually see Caroline's little webbed fingers!"

Michael smiled, face muscles twitching painfully.

Make that two more minutes.

7:56 P.M.

"*Caroline.*" Amy stood outside the upstairs bathroom, knocking lightly but insistently on the door. "*Caroline!*"

"What," Caroline's voice called back bleakly from within.

"You know what. Get out of this bathroom and go downstairs. *Now.*"

"I can't."

"You better," Amy warned. "Mom's down there with Michael, and it's *not pretty.*"

"*How* not pretty?"

"I have two words for you: *baby pictures.*"

There was a jingling in the lock, and the bathroom door opened a crack. An angry blue-gray eye peeked out. "*Amy!* You said you would protect him from her!"

"I tried, I tried. But you know Mom—" Amy blinked, gawking at her sister. "Caroline . . . your hair . . ."

"I know," Caroline muttered dejectedly, hanging her head in shame. "I tried brushing it out, but that just made it worse."

"No, no, no." Amy exhaled. "It's amazing!"

Caroline snorted, staring at the floor. "You mean it's *big*."

"No, I don't. I mean it's *gorgeous!*" Amy took a step backward into the hall to get the full-length view. "Oh, Caroline," she whispered, placing her hand over her heart. "Everything *about* you is gorgeous. . . ."

Caroline looked up, her eyes glistening. "You really mean it?"

Amy rushed forward, seizing her younger sister by the elbows. "Listen to me, Caroline, and listen good: Right now you look better than you have *ever* looked in your *entire life*. And I can think of a hundred good reasons why you should be racing down those stairs to see Michael, not the least of which is sitting beside him *as we speak,* showing him photos of your naked baby butt." Amy let go of her sister's arms and backed up into the hall. *"Okay?"* she asked, holding out her hand.

Caroline sniffled, dabbed at her nose with a crumpled tissue, and nodded. "Okay." She tossed away the tissue and stepped out of the bathroom, taking her sister's hand.

As Amy led her down the hall, Caroline turned to her, worried. "Mom's not *really* showing him my baby pictures—is she?"

"You should be happy that's *all* she's showing

him," Amy replied. "Jim got my whole medical history."

7:58 P.M.

". . . would you believe in a million years that teeth could grow so crooked?" Mrs. Knapp asked, holding the x rays up to the ceiling light so that Michael could get a good look.

Michael shook his head and said in unison with Dr. Knapp, "Not in a million years."

"Mother!"

Michael turned to see Caroline's sister stepping into the living room. "Could I see you in the kitchen for a moment?" she asked sweetly, approaching the sofa.

"Not right now, Amy, dear," Mrs. Knapp said, waving her daughter away. "I'm right in the middle of showing our guest, Michael here, some of Caroline's—"

"Oh—but I *insist.*" Amy grabbed her mother's hand, jerked the woman to her feet, and briskly hauled her out of the room.

Michael was left sitting on the couch, alone in the living room with Dr. Knapp, who was now snoring loudly from his seat in the corner.

Michael let out a slow, shaky breath. *This isn't too weird,* he tried to convince himself.

Glancing down, he saw that he was still clutching

143

the glass jar Mrs. Knapp had given him to hold. He held it up now, tilting it, and Caroline's baby teeth rattled to one side like twenty tiny dice.

Okay. Forget what I just said. This is very, very weird.

"Hey, Redmonster."

Michael spun to see Caroline standing in the entranceway. He leaped to his feet. Caroline was *stunning*.

"Hey, Knapsack," he managed.

She crossed over to him, smiling apologetically. "Sorry I took so long."

Michael had planned to say, Don't be sorry—it was worth the wait, but he only got as far as "Don't" before the speech center of his brain completely shut down.

Her dress was even more fantastic than he remembered, but it was nothing compared to the rest of her. Her light brown hair, usually pulled back in a ponytail, now framed her face in thick, loose ringlets that just reached the top of her bare shoulders. Her blue-gray eyes must have stolen some of the violet from her dress because they sparkled like amethysts under smoky eyelids and thick, dark lashes. Her skin was glowing, and the pearls in her ears and around her neck could barely match the radiance of her smile.

He had no idea he could even *think* like that.

"Don't what?" Caroline asked.

". . . worry about it," Michael finished, finally regaining the use of his mouth. He gestured at the stack of photo albums on the sofa. "I was, uh, kept pretty busy."

"Oh God." Caroline winced. "Did my mom show you all those?"

Michael shrugged. "It was that or the home videos."

The clock on the mantel started chiming.

"Eight o'clock," Michael announced, checking his watch. "I guess this means we're now officially late."

"*Fashionably* late," Caroline corrected.

"*Very* fashionably," Michael added, his gaze falling on her dress once more. Now that she stood close to him, he could see that her velvet bodice was embroidered with a subtle, quilted flower pattern. He suddenly remembered the corsage he'd brought with him. "Here—this is for you."

Caroline glanced at the item he was extending toward her. "Oh, Michael. A jar of teeth. How thoughtful."

"Oops—sorry." Michael quickly set the jar down on the coffee table and scooped up the plastic container that he'd placed there. "I mean . . . *this* is for you."

Caroline took the clear case and opened it, removing the delicate blossom from within. The creamy white flower was pinned to a long, violet ribbon.

"It's an orchid," Michael told her, reaching for it. "Here, let me. . . ." Taking the corsage from her, he centered the blossom above her left hand, then wrapped the satin ribbon gently and firmly around her wrist, securing it with a bow. "There."

Caroline held out her hand, admiring the result. "Thank you," she said, her voice soft and sincere. "It's gorgeous." She smiled once again, raising her eyes to his.

"Uh . . . do you want to leave now?" Michael asked her.

"Do I *want* to leave now?" Caroline replied. "Try *desperately need to.* In fact, I'll race you to the car."

They were halfway out the front door when Michael stopped short. "Wait—shouldn't we say good-bye to your mother?"

Caroline considered the suggestion for a half second, then nodded. "You're right." Turning around, she hollered, *"Bye, Mom! We're leaving!"* Then she strong-armed Michael outside and slammed the door shut behind them.

"Keep your fingers crossed," Michael said, his breath fogging in the night air. "Suzie doesn't like the cold weather. If she's still being difficult, we may end up *walking* to the dance."

Caroline was holding on to his arm to keep from slipping on the icy driveway. Now he felt her fingers tense up through his sleeve. "Who's Suzie?" she asked.

"*That's* Suzie," Michael said, pointing to the car parked at the curb. "She's a—"

A pair of headlights suddenly beamed on from a car parked down the street, then the vehicle lurched toward them with two honks. He grabbed

Caroline's arm—instinctively, protectively—as they were swept by the twin yellow beams. The car pulled alongside them.

The driver leaned out his window. "Good evening," he said cordially, tipping a chauffeur's cap. "I'm here to escort a Mr. Michael Redmont and his date, Caroline, to the holiday dance."

Michael couldn't move. He couldn't speak. He just stood there, rooted to the ground, feeling like he was about to drop dead from shock.

"Oh, Michael . . . ," Caroline uttered, staring in awe at the huge, classic automobile that idled before them, gleaming like white marble in the moonlight. "I can't believe you rented a Rolls!"

It took a moment for Michael to find his voice. When he did, he could barely squeak out his four-word reply: "That's not a Rolls. . . ."

8:17 P.M.

"It's a supercharged, 320-horsepower, Model SJ Duesenberg Rollston convertible sedan, built in Paris in 1936 by the legendary auto designer Dutch Darrin. I won it off a British army general in a game of five-card stud."

As Michael's grandfather spoke to her over the rhythmic purr of the motor, Caroline leaned back into the rich, red leather backseat. It was as wide and soft as a sofa. And deep: Her feet barely touched the floor.

Michael leaned toward her and said, "Don't believe a word out of the old coot's mouth, Caroline. Gramps told *me* he got this car from a French opera singer who traded it to him for a crate of peanut butter and a bottle of whiskey."

"That's right—I *did* tell you that," his grandfather cut in. "And which do you think's more incredible, Caroline: *that* story or the fact that Mikey here believed it?" He winked at her in the rearview mirror.

Caroline laughed. "Oh, Michael's gullibility never ceases to amaze me." She turned to her seat partner. "But *really*, Michael," she told him in an admonishing tone of voice, "*everyone* knows opera singers don't eat peanut butter. It's too hard to sing all those high notes with their tongues stuck to the roofs of their mouths."

Behind the wheel Gramps chuckled heartily, then tossed his grandson a meaningful look. "Just 'one of the guys'—huh, Mikey?"

Michael emitted a high, weak-sounding laugh.

Caroline felt like she'd just missed something. "What guys?" she asked.

Michael's bow tie must have been too tight because now he hooked a finger inside his collar and gave it a couple of tugs. "It's nothing," he told her. "Just a little joke that Gramps and I, uh—*oh, look!*" He stabbed his finger out her window toward the high school, nearly decking her in the process. *"We're here!"*

Nine

8:20 P.M.

"WOW . . . I DON'T believe it," Caroline said. Standing next to her, Michael could only nod in agreement. They'd both stopped in their tracks immediately inside the doorway to the cafeteria, staring around in dumbstruck amazement.

The decorating committee had truly outdone themselves.

The familiar, pea green cinder-block walls had been entirely concealed behind the huge sheets of black paper. These were now festooned with elaborate, gold-foil cutouts shaped like large Mardi Gras masks, which seemed to float in the darkness like exotic, glittering butterflies.

The cafeteria tables had vanished as well. In their place cloth-covered banquette tables had been arranged around the perimeter of the room, each sporting a festive bouquet of balloons. More balloons had been strung together to form huge, purple-and-gold arches that vaulted the dance floor like helium-filled rainbows. Above them crepe-paper streamers were interspersed with strings of white Christmas-tree lights that twinkled down from the ceiling like a starry sky.

The entire room seemed to be revolving around a giant, glittering mirror ball that cast off countless palm-sized reflections in a dizzy carousel of colored light. They swept the room like a million tiny searchlights, swimming over the tables, the walls, and the many students crowding the dance floor.

Michael drew an anxious breath. For some reason it felt a little strange to be arriving with the dance already in progress like this. Now that he and Caroline were finally there, he couldn't shake the feeling that they were intruding on some private, exclusive affair. It felt like they were gate-crashers, like they hadn't been invited. Like at any moment someone was going to step up to them and say—

"You two can't stay here."

The loud, stern voice made them both jump.

Mr. McMinnaman, the hall monitor–science teacher from hell, was standing in the hallway behind them, his hands on his hips.

"We can't?" Caroline asked.

"Absolutely not," the teacher replied curtly.

"But—," Michael began.

"These doorways have to stay clear of traffic,"

the thin older man explained. "In or out. Which is it going to be?"

For a second neither Michael nor Caroline could respond. Then—together—they sighed, blurted, "In," and moved quickly through the doors and away from the sour-faced man.

They'd gotten several yards before Michael's brain finally registered what it had just seen.

No way . . .

He stopped dead in his tracks, pivoting slowly on his heels. No, his eyes *hadn't* been playing tricks.

"Hey, Mr. McMinnaman," he called back to the man guarding the doorway. "That's a really great tux."

The older man's eyes narrowed in suspicion behind their thick lenses. "Thank you."

"I could be mistaken," Michael said, "but isn't that the *El Dorado?*"

"Why, yes—yes, it is," he answered proudly, giving each of his yellow velveteen cuffs a crisp tug.

"*Very* snazzy," Michael replied before turning away.

11:39 P.M.

After dancing for most of the evening Caroline and Michael decided to sit out a few songs and catch their breath. They rested at a banquette table, listening to Xenophobic Linguistics perform their final set of the evening.

On the dance floor in front of them couples bounced and gyrated to the music—another of the band's original, reggae-style numbers. Behind his drum set the Rat was seriously cutting loose. His bow tie hung down from his open collar, and his long brown hair was damp with perspiration.

While Caroline normally would have thought it absurd that a high-school band from Ohio was playing Jamaican music at a winter formal, it somehow seemed in keeping with the rest of the evening's absurdities. *Forget Mardi Gras Magic,* she thought. *Tonight's theme should have been Believe It or Not!* Nothing seemed to fit in the normal scheme of things.

For one thing, Mason Parker—who'd been voted King of the Winter Dance (surprise, surprise)—*wasn't* dancing with his queen, Cecily Vaughn. And the unofficially named Class Nerd, the Trauther, and his surprising date, Liza Wilde, hadn't danced once. Very strange. Liza was boogying it up with the usually reserved foreign-exchange student.

Of course, perhaps the freakiest thing of all was the fact that Caroline herself was there and having fun. She—Caroline Knapp, aka Knapsack. At the winter dance for the first time in her life. And wearing a *dress,* not a garbage bag.

Caroline smiled to herself. To think that only a few hours ago she'd been wearing air fresheners instead of orchids. She looked down at her wrist.

"So tell me, Mikey. Was purple just a lucky guess?" she asked.

Michael looked at her over the rim of a plastic cup. "Purple?"

Caroline held up her left hand, indicating the corsage he'd so carefully tied around her wrist more than three hours ago. "The ribbon, the orchid. They go perfectly with my dress. But you didn't know I'd be wearing this color when you got it for me. Right?"

Michael downed his punch. "Actually," he said, "I have a small confession to make, Knapsack. I saw you trying that dress on in the mall this afternoon."

"You saw me . . . ?" Caroline repeated, her voice fading as her brain did an automatic rewind.

She remembered her mother asking if she knew the boys who were outside the dress shop. *Was Michael one of them?* Apparently so.

A millisecond later—with a sensation like dominoes toppling over in her mind—Caroline pieced together exactly what must have happened:

How Michael must have seen her in the bridesmaid dress and assumed she was buying it for tonight. How he must have figured she'd misunderstood his original plans to go in gag outfits. How—not wanting to hurt her feelings—he must have had to rush around to get the corsage, rent his tux, and make plans for his grandfather to be their chauffeur.

Caroline could feel a prickly warmth rising in her cheeks and ears but wasn't sure whether she was

153

blushing because she was flattered or because she was appalled.

On the one hand, it was really sweet that Michael would go to all that trouble for her. On the other, if it had all been done just to protect her feelings, did that mean everything about tonight—all the dancing, the laughing, every single second of the past three hours—had been a great big *lie?*

Her next thought made her blood run cold: *I've been acting like one of the people Michael wanted us to ridicule.*

Trying to keep her voice steady, Caroline said, "It's bogus, isn't it?"

Michael was idly fingering the strands of Mardi Gras beads that hung around his neck. He stopped and looked at her. "What is?"

She gestured around, trying to inject a gleeful snicker into her voice. "Everything. This dance, the people. Everything."

Michael reached over and grabbed her cup, sniffing its contents. "All right, Knapsack. Just what punch bowl are *you* drinking from?"

Caroline ignored him. "I mean, if you ask me, a dance is just a pathetic attempt to manufacture romance. It's bad enough when someone isn't asked to go and feels like an outcast. But do the couples who go really have it any better?" She nodded at the dance floor. "Just look at some of them. All dressed up, thinking they've found true love. Do they really think it's *real?* That any of it's going to *last?* Spare me."

Michael was quiet. After a moment he said,

"Who can say? You said yourself that your sister and her boyfriend went to one of these dances. And they're still together, right?"

"Yeah. But that was, like, a one-in-a-million occurrence."

Michael looked down in his lap. "I don't know. I kinda like to think lightning can strike twice in the same place. . . . Don't you?"

His tone was flippant, but when he looked back up at her, his expression was strangely serious. He stared her in the eyes—seemed to search them, to look *through* them—as if the answer to his question could be found somewhere in their depths. Caroline returned his gaze, swallowed hard, and was about to reply . . .

. . . when Michael crossed his eyes and stuck his tongue out at her.

"Gotcha," he said, snorting. Then he shrugged. "The way I figure, if I find true love, I find it. But I'm not gonna waste my time looking for it, *that's* for sure."

Onstage, Xenophobic Linguistics finished their song, and Michael turned away from her to applaud. Caroline kept her eyes on him a moment longer before joining in the applause herself.

When the clapping stopped, Ira Berg leaned in close to the mike. "And now," he announced in a mock-sultry voice, "a little something to put you all in the holiday spirit."

The Rat began tapping a mellow beat on his cymbals, the bass and guitars strummed a familiar intro, and Ira began to croon: *"Chestnuts roasting on an open fire . . ."*

Caroline thought she heard Michael groan. But when she glanced at him out of the corner of her eye, he seemed to be all right. He was simply watching the couples swaying on the dance floor in front of them, his hands resting comfortably on his lap. Their knees were about half a foot apart.

She suddenly had to know.

Pretending to watch the stage, Caroline nonchalantly placed her own hands in her lap. Then, taking a breath, she slowly—*very* slowly—began inching her leg toward his.

A moment later their knees touched and the back of their hands met, knuckles grazing together—casually, carelessly—as if it were happening by accident.

Michael didn't flinch or pull away.

Not even a little.

Claude
&
Liza

by
Elizabeth Skurnick

One

Claude

I T WAS MY last day at Riverside High School.

My last day in America.

My last day ever to see the girl I'd had a crush on since arriving at the start of the fall term three months ago, in September.

Crush.

Americans had no idea how funny their slang could sound to foreigners like me.

But *crush* did seem like a good word to describe the feeling I got whenever I saw Liza Wilde, considering that it crushed me to be too shy to talk to her. Even now, as she stood just a few feet away at her own locker, I couldn't imagine just walking up to her.

But today was my last opportunity.

Fat chance of my taking it.

That American expression reminded me of my

first day at Riverside, and I turned my sidelong glance from Liza's beautiful face to my almost empty locker. I'd never forget how when Tom Trauth, aka "the Trauther" (my host brother), had introduced me to our homeroom class, a guy seated in the front row had burst out with, "Yo, dude, those jeans are *phat!*"

I'd looked down to see if I'd gained any weight on the plane from Belgium to America.

The foreign-student exchange program had been my mother's idea since she herself had studied in Belgium during her last year of medical school and had a blast (another word I picked up at Riverside). My American mom had clapped eyes on my Belgian dad, and it was love at first sight. At least that was what my father used to say before he died two years ago.

That was something I didn't want to think about—ever. In fact, it was pretty much the reason my mom thought I should get away from home for a while. Breathe some fresh air, she'd said. I'd been worried about leaving my mom (she likes me to call her the American "Mom" instead of *Maman,* as the French say) all alone. But my uncle Antoine had handed me a new suitcase and promised to take good care of her while I was away: "As good care as you do, Claude."

Then, just a few weeks later, we'd met my host father, Frank Trauth, who'd been on a business trip to Belgium at the time. Mr. Trauth and my mother had contacted the agency on the same day, so they'd thought it was fate that we be paired.

We'd met Mr. Trauth at a quiet café near my house. Huge, with a beaming red face and big ham hands, Mr. Trauth had burst into the café and boomed, "Miz Delpy? Glad to meetcha!" Next he smacked me on the back so hard, I spit out my coffee, then smacked my *mother* on the back too.

And when I'd gotten off the plane in America, the Trauths had been lined up at the gate with a big sign that read Welcome, Claude! and a bunch of balloons. I'd recognized Tom (the one my age) right away from the family pictures Mrs. Trauth had sent us. Redheaded, tall, skinny, with huge ears, he looked exactly like a large-sized Howdy Doody. Terry, his little brother, looked like a mini-Tom. And Mrs. Trauth was just as big and beaming as her husband.

I liked them all right away.

During the drive to their house Terry had given me one of the Beanie Babies. Once home, Tom had shown me the room we'd share—a cavelike den with *Star Wars* memorabilia and shots of Kate Winslet pasted all over the walls. He'd handed me a wallet-sized, well-preserved photo from *Titanic* cut out from a magazine. Looking at me very seriously, he'd said, "Don't ever forget the goddess, Claude."

Mrs. Trauth, a wedding planner, had run up and down the stairs with caterer's samples for us to taste, lifting our shirts and yelling, "You're both too skinny!" And I got used to Mr. Trauth's slaps on the back once I learned to hold my breath before he did it.

But I'd had *no* idea what to expect from my American classmates. All I had to go on were the dubbed overseas versions of shows like *Saved by the Bell* and *Beverly Hills 90210* plus some old pictures of my mother in a polyester pantsuit and platform shoes at a school dance in the 1970s. Really accurate, huh?

In Belgium, I'd attended the International School, which was full of wealthy diplomats' kids who partied and shopped more than they studied. With their expensively cut hair and couture wardrobes, all the girls looked like models, and all the guys carried cell phones they talked on constantly—usually to someone in another classroom.

Needless to say, as the son of two local doctors at the university hospital (compared to the kids of film directors, billionaires, and diplomats, with their chauffeurs and ten-room flats), I was at the bottom of the totem pole in terms of "cool." My mother liked the school because I'd meet kids from all over and would learn to speak flawless English, German, and French. I got the languages down, but I still never had much to say to my classmates.

I had a lot to say, though, to my classmates at Riverside, who I liked very much; I was just too shy to say any of it.

Now, as I collected my books from my locker and watched the Trauther clown around with some guys from chemistry class, I felt a little choked up about leaving.

After tonight's winter formal I'd pack up, and tomorrow morning I'd fly home for *Noël* (Christmas). I was definitely going to miss the warmth and buzz of the Trauth family homestead.

And I was definitely going to miss looking at Liza Wilde from Monday through Friday.

I'd noticed her that first day at Riverside. She and a group of girls had been standing around talking by the lockers when a guy who reminded me of the jerks at my old school walked up to her and put his arm around her.

She'd shot away from him fast, and then she and one of the girls headed down the hall toward where Tom and I were standing. As the two girls neared me and Tom, I saw the other girl look back at the guy and snicker. "Did somebody just say *loser?*" she asked.

It had taken Tom quite a while to explain that phrase to me.

"Who's that guy with the big pants?" I'd asked Tom.

"The 'loser' is Ira Berg. He's the lead singer for Xenophobic Linguistics." Tom made little quote marks with his fingers as he said the last two words.

Liza, whose name I hadn't known that day, looked directly at me for a moment as she walked down the hall. When our eyes met, I suddenly forgot everything: losing my father, the new school, the fact that I had just taken a plane halfway around the world. . . .

As I'd stared at her, the tall brunette with the golden tan and the slow, curving smile, I was very glad I'd taken my mother's advice to come to America.

Okay, so maybe it was kind of superficial to have a big crush on a girl just because she was so pretty. But I'd sensed that first day that there was more to Liza Wilde than her looks. As the weeks and months passed, watching her with her friends or heading to the tennis courts with her racket, I'd

163

noticed she was friendly, smart, and interesting—all without ever having said one word to her.

And unless I suddenly got a truckful of guts, I'd spend my last day at Riverside in the same position I'd spent my first day: crazy about a girl I was too chicken to talk to. (Now, there was a slang word I had no trouble understanding.)

It wasn't that I hadn't had a girlfriend before. Last year my friend Jacques's sister Mireille and I had dated for a couple of months. And the summer before my father died, I'd met an Italian girl, Lucrezia, who'd spent June and July improving my accent—and kisses—while I showed her around my city. At the time I'd felt like I was crazy about both of them. But now I knew what I'd felt had just been doggie love (or was that puppy love?) compared to what happened when I just *looked* at Liza.

And now, right this very minute, here she was, mere feet from me—and not even surrounded by her pack of friends. I still couldn't say a word.

"Ready, buddy boy?" Tom asked me.

Liza was the captain of the girls' tennis team. She was in all the high-level English and math courses.

"Claude?" Tom asked again.

Oh, and did I forget to mention that with her large, brown eyes and chestnut hair always swept up into a tight ponytail, she was also heart-stoppingly beautiful?

I felt a pinch on my arm. "Time to wake up." Tom grinned at me. He was always grinning.

I'd never told Tom about my crush on Liza. I

guess because it felt so private to me. I just didn't go around talking about my feelings. And that, I'd discovered, was universal among guys.

"Well, we sure are going to miss how talkative you are!" Tom boomed. Around us, people began to laugh. I felt my face flush, then mock-punched Tom. Three lockers away I could *feel* Liza turn and look at me. Her friends were giggling.

Looking at Tom and me, who wouldn't giggle? A gangly (but lovable) nerd and a pale guy with a funny accent and wire-rimmed glasses. Oh yeah, I was prime dating material.

Did somebody just say *loser?*

Two

Liza

DIVORCE. DEFINITELY ONE of the ugliest words in the English language. I knew divorce was sort of common these days, but did *everyone's* parents pretend they loved each other for twenty years, then agree they hadn't really had anything to say for nineteen of those years?

Did *everyone's* parents put the family house on the market so both of them could go back to school and get the degrees they never finished because of the birth of their little baby girl? (That'd be me.)

And did *everyone's* parents talk about how *now* their lives could start, how *now* they felt in control of their destinies, how *now* they could concentrate on what they really wanted?

And did *every* kid of divorcing parents feel like the shortest, littlest bleep on the radar screen of life?

You just have to concentrate on your own life now, Liza.

My best friend, Serena, made that suggestion. She's a sweetie, but she's watched one too many episodes of *Days of Our Lives.*

Put it all into your game, Wilde.

That was from my tennis coach, Paige Hatchett. Like I even felt like *playing* the game.

Honey, we're going to be just like college roommates!

You guessed it: Mom. And she was dreaming as usual.

Honeybuns, what you don't understand yet is that this separation will actually strengthen my relationship with your mother.

Dad, could you spell *c-o-n-d-e-s-c-e-n-d-i-n-g?*

It was back in July that my parents announced they were getting a divorce, and for the past five months I've had no one to talk to about it, no one who seems to understand. So when Ira Berg started asking me out in September, I must have been so upset about my parents that I lost all my powers of discrimination.

That *had* to be the reason why I'd actually agreed to go out with him.

He was cute—well, cute from five feet away—and the lead singer in this rock band called the Xenophobic Linguistics, which should have told me something right there. During the drive to the burger place (our first and last date) I'd tried to make small talk, but Ira had turned the music up louder, opened a pack of Camel cigarettes, and grinned at me.

"Cool, huh?" he said, rocking his chin to the

music and blowing disgusting smoke in my face.

"Yeah, really cool," I muttered.

Over cheeseburgers, fries, and sodas Ira became even more charming. "You're pretty," he said, "but you'd be prettier if you'd loosen up. You know, be less serious all the time."

What a jerk.

"You weren't around this summer, sexy," Ira said next, reaching across the table to grab my hand. "Or I'd have asked you out before."

* "My parents were filing for *divorce*," I snapped at him. "I was staying with my grandparents a lot— things were pretty tense at home. Still are . . ." I pulled my hand away from his and started shredding my napkin. Talking about it brought all my feelings to the surface.

Ira got up and slid next to me in the booth. He put his arm around me, which I took for a gesture of comfort.

Wrong.

Tears stung my eyes. "It's really tough," I choked out, then had to stifle a sob. "But—"

"But *I* know how to make you feel better," Ira said before popping one of my french fries into his mouth.

"Are you gonna eat those?" He gestured at the fries untouched on my plate and poured a blob of ketchup on them even though I hadn't responded. He stuffed a few fries in his mouth, wiped his lips with a napkin, then repeated, "I really do know how to make you feel better."

And then I'd felt his greasy lips nuzzling my neck.

168

I screamed.

Honest to God, I screamed. A loud, long scream. Ira jumped out of the booth, looking at me with horror. "Are you *nuts?*" he hissed.

Ira's greasy kiss, his overpowering cologne, my parents' divorce—of course I'd gone mental.

The waitresses gathered around to ask if I was all right. Ira yelled that I was sick and that he was going to call my mother to come get me. After he called, we waited outside together, and then he put his arm around me *again.* I glared at him, and he went back to sucking on his cigarettes.

When my parents—yes, *both* of them—had arrived, I'd sat in a stony silence the whole way home. For the first time in months they hadn't tried to sweet-talk, pep-talk, or tough-love-talk me out of it. My mother had turned around a lot to give me concerned looks, and my father had uttered a couple of deep sighs.

The next day I'd headed for the courts to slam balls against the backboard while I desperately tried not to feel like I'd lost touch with the gravitational pull of the earth and was spinning off wildly into the stratosphere.

Tennis, anyone?

So, that was pretty much why I was blowing off the winter formal tonight. Serena had been bugging me about going for weeks, but I was dead set against it. Aside from my inability to have any fun anymore, the thought of yakking couples, strings of Mardi Gras beads (Mardi Gras was the so-called theme), and fake po'-boy sandwiches made with cafeteria mystery meat didn't sound even remotely like a good time.

Now, as I stuffed my books in my backpack, I sneaked a peek at Claude Delpy, the foreign-exchange student. Sometimes just looking at him—with his good posture, cute face, and polite demeanor—could make me feel a little bit better. I'd noticed him when he first arrived, but he seemed pretty shy. And after the Ira Berg experience I wasn't giving anyone the benefit of the doubt by speaking to them first.

Tom Trauth was suddenly standing an inch away from me.

"Uh, Liza, do you by any chance have a date for the dance tonight?"

Tom's been kind of a joker since before I can remember. In third grade he used to stuff corn up his nose at lunch. Last Halloween he dressed up as Xena, Warrior Princess. So I was all prepared to give him a joking answer.

"Tom . . . " I began, wishing I actually still had a sense of humor. But then I felt a familiar weight. It was Ira Berg, draping his skinny arm around my shoulders—again.

"I'd *love* to go with you!" I heard myself practically shouting to the guy known as the Trauther.

Tom raised one eyebrow higher than I'd ever seen anyone manage, then grinned and pumped his fist in the air with a silent *yes!*

I smiled back. Ira took his arm from around me as if I were a leper, looked at me as if I were something on the bottom of his shoe, then trundled off

170

down the hall, his big jeans catching on the soles of his combat boots.

"Awesome! Mission accomplished!" said the Trauther. "How 'bout we meet in front of the caf at eight?"

Mission accomplished is right, I seconded mentally. *The Berg blocker has been activated.* "Sounds good, Tom."

When I got home, it was business as usual. I came into the front hallway, which was now filled with boxes and tape. I felt tears rise in my throat. Would anything ever be the same again?

"Honey?" I heard my mother calling from upstairs. "Honey? Is that you?"

I couldn't take it. I ran back out into the cool December afternoon, the tears now rising in my eyes. I threw my workout bag onto my bike and headed to the courts. Everyone would have gone home from practice, I knew, and I would have the courts all to myself. And even though I was sick of myself, I was the best company I had right now.

"Get used to it, Wilde," I told myself as I pumped the pedals. "Get used to it."

Three

Claude

ALL TOM HAD talked about the whole way home was how he couldn't believe Liza Wilde had been dateless for the formal. Since he'd yapped and yapped about it, I'd been saved from trying to croak out a "you go, guy," or whatever was the right expression.

When we walked through the front door, I actually had to stop myself from kicking it repeatedly.

So Tom liked Liza too. Why hadn't I seen it? And more important, why hadn't he said anything to me?

Well, that was easily answered. Why hadn't I said anything to him?

We were both shy guys. Tom hid behind a joking veneer, and I hid behind my glasses.

"Hey, Claude." Tom turned to me with begging

eyes. "You gotta help me. I've got only four hours to learn how to dance!"

I thought of Liza and the way her eyes had sparkled when she'd turned around and told Tom she'd love to go to the formal with him.

I clenched my fists. I was going to be happy for my Tom, even if it killed me.

"You bet, Tom." That was a phrase Mr. Trauth used when he was talking to an irate customer on the phone.

The dance lesson consisted mostly of Tom twirling around the living room while I tried not to show how depressed I was. Terry even joined us, doing a line dance he'd learned in school.

"And Claude," Tom said, huffing and puffing, "you have to teach me some romantic French phrases. How do you say, 'You look really beautiful tonight'?"

I swallowed. *"Ce soir, comme toujours, tu es la fille la plus belle dans tout le monde."*

"Michelle, *ma belle* . . . " Terry began to hum.

"Great, man! Thanks!" Tom told me, twirling Terry around. "Liza's gonna love it!"

"Tom, uh, I think I'm going to head out for a run," I told him. "You just keep practicing. You're doing great."

"Don't take too long." Tom looked at his over-sized watch, which had more features than my laptop. "I need you to help me figure out which shirt to wear with my new suit. Plus you'll need to figure out what to wear too."

I froze, one hand on the doorknob.

"What do you mean?" I asked. "Why would I be going? You're the only one with the hot date." I'd never said anything truer.

He stared at me, his mouth hanging open, his eyes opened wide. He rushed over to me and put both hands on either of my shoulders. "Claude, buddy, you've gotta come! You've gotta help me! Coach me on what to say, how to say it, what dance to do when. I've never taken a girl to a dance before."

Now it was my turn to stare at him.

"Claude—this is *Liza Wilde* we're talking about. You've gotta help me! Please? Pretty please? Pleeeeeeeeeeeeeese!"

The knife dug a little deeper, twisted a little harder. But how could I tell Tom no? He'd been a great friend to me these past three months.

"Okay, Tom," I told him. "I'll go. It *is* my last night here, so I might as well go to say good-bye to everyone." *Yeah, like that would ever happen.*

He pumped his fist in the air. "Yes!"

"I'll be back soon." I couldn't open the door fast enough.

"Thanks, Claude." Tom slapped me on the back just like his father always did. "You're the man."

I took a different path than usual from the Trauths', toward the area of town that was dotted with parks and playgrounds.

I hadn't felt this bad, this lost, since my father had died and my mother and I had returned from the hospital to the empty apartment.

"Don't lose it now, Claude," I panted.

I forced myself into a sprint. The faster I ran, the less I would have to think about Tom or Liza. Tom and Liza dancing. Arg! My heart pounding, I raced down a small slope and stopped myself on the chain-link fence of some tennis courts, putting my fingers though the holes and leaning over while I tried to catch my breath.

"You okay?" asked a girl's voice.

I looked up, but my glasses were so steamed, I couldn't see in front of me. I pulled off the wire rims, wiped them on my shirt, and called back, "Yeah, thanks, just catching my—"

Breath.

Now that I had vision again, all my powers of speech left me.

The girl talking to me was Liza Wilde.

"Your what?" she asked, twirling her tennis racket. Her beautiful face was flushed from exertion, and in front of her I saw the barrage of tennis balls she'd evidently directed fiercely across the court.

"I—" *Speak, Claude.* "Just taking a breather."

"I could use a major breather," she said, gesturing at all the tennis balls. Then in a lower voice she added, "Maybe *I* should just go run instead of slamming more balls. Yeah, run away from *home.*" She looked down at the ground. For a second I thought she might even cry.

"Can I ask why?" I ventured.

Liza darted up her head. "You're staying with Tom Trauth's family, right?"

175

So, she wanted to talk about Tom. I nodded. "By the way, I think we're the only two people who call him *Tom*."

Liza laughed. Maybe I'd been wrong in thinking she was going to cry. "I don't like calling him the Trauther. It's, well, kind of disrespectful, you know? I like Tom a lot. Always have."

I like Tom a lot. Always have.

Could that knife plunge in any deeper?

"So where are you from?" she asked.

"Bruxelles," I said automatically. "Belgium."

"Et vous appelez Claude, oui?" Liza was smiling.

She knew my name. And she'd said it in French.

"Oui. Your accent is very good," I told her, hating how boring I sounded.

"So's yours," she said, and we both laughed. She picked up a tennis ball and began bouncing it with the flat of her racket, her eyes on the movement. "My parents are getting divorced," she suddenly said. "That's what I meant before about running away."

"I'm very sorry to hear that," I offered. "That's a lot to deal with."

Liza looked up. "Are your parents divorced?"

"No," I said, trying not to sound too emotional. "My father . . . died . . . a couple of years ago. I know what it's like to have your family torn apart. To feel like you have no control."

Liza put down her racket. I was worried she was going to get all sympathetic and concerned-eyed like people always did, but she just nodded, her expression grave. "I'm really sorry, Claude. *That's* a lot to deal with."

We looked at each other for a moment, and I had the feeling she felt the same way I did: that a little bond had formed between us. A bond of understanding between two people who'd never said two words to each other before now.

"So, um, are you going to the dance?" Liza asked.

"Yeah, I've been drafted."

"Well, I guess I'll see you there, then," she said.

I guessed that meant she wanted me to leave. "Yeah," I called with a stupid, frozen smile as I started jogging away. "I'll see you there."

But she was already slamming balls across the court.

I ran home faster than I'd ever run before.

Pure adrenaline.

On my very last day in America, I'd finally talked to the girl of my dreams.

And during my very last night she'd be dancing in the arms of my very good friend.

Four

Liza

"*I*'M DRESSING YOU—and doing your hair and makeup," Serena insisted as I stood fresh from the shower with a towel wrapped around me in her bedroom. I looked at the alarm clock on her bedside table. Two hours till I'd meet Tom at the party.

Till I'd see Claude again.

After he ran off, I'd actually *felt* his absence. It wasn't like we'd talked for very long, but we had *talked*. Really talked. I'd stayed at the courts for about another half hour, not slamming the balls as hard. I'd felt better, and I didn't understand why until I realized *why* was exactly the answer.

Claude had asked me *why* when I'd casually said I wanted to run away from home. He hadn't told me how I should feel or what I should do about it; he'd just asked *why*.

"This is it!" Serena exclaimed, snapping me out of my thoughts. She held a long, slinky, sleeveless red dress in one hand and a pair of red sandals in the other. "You're gonna look amazing!"

I doubted that, but Serena hadn't been named Most School Spirit for nothing.

She, of course, was already dressed and looked incredible. With her long, dark curls, huge, blue eyes, and iridescent toenails peeking out of her metallic slides, she'd look great in anything. But wearing a floor-length, ice blue skirt with a spangled gauze overlay and a silvery, satiny tank top, she looked drop-dread gorgeous.

"Liza, I don't get why you don't do something with yourself every day," Serena said, laying the dress and shoes on the bed. "I mean, lose the ponytail and those loose jeans and T-shirts already!" She sat down at her vanity to stroke on mascara.

"You know getting all dressed up isn't me," I told her. "I can't even imagine wearing that dress."

Serena stuck the mascara wand back in the tube and twisted the cap. She got down on her hands and knees. "*Please,* Liza—let me help you!" she implored, gesturing wildly.

I laughed. "Okay, okay. I'm all yours."

Serena beamed and stood up, slid three steel butterfly pins into her hair, gave herself a final once-over, and turned to me. "This won't hurt a bit."

"Wow," Serena said, her mouth hanging open.
"Wow," I echoed, almost unable to believe the

girl staring back at me in the mirror *was* me.

"The Trauther's gonna have a heart attack when he sees you." Tom! I had completely forgotten about him. The minute I'd accepted his invitation in the hallway at school, the vision of a pain-free night with my goofy elementary-school buddy had risen through my mind and disappeared like bubbles in 7UP. I doubted that Tom had asked me to the dance because he had a crush on me or anything. I figured he just wanted a pain-free date himself. Or just a date, period.

Staring into the mirror, I had to admit that the transformation was amazing. Serena had blow-dried my hair (I usually just let it air dry) and put tons of weird-looking gunk in it so that it was sleek and smooth, like a model's. And using only the teensiest bit of eye shadow, mascara, and lip gloss (I'd watched her like a hawk), she had transformed my face from boring to actually *glowing*.

And the dress! I had no idea that a dress could make me look like a completely different person. The slinky red thing had spaghetti straps and was embroidered with tiny red flowers across the top. And since Serena and I wore the same size shoes, the red sandals fit perfectly. The dress clung in all the right places without being so revealing that I felt uncomfortable.

I was glad I looked like a completely different person. For a night, that was just what I needed.

"Liza, this is why you make me so mad," Serena said. "I have to work really hard at myself, but you could look this good *all the time.*"

"I don't think putting on lip gloss and a few barrettes

qualifies as *really hard*," I said, laughing. "But I think you've definitely worked a magic trick here."

"Well, you're lucky the Ira-Berg-that-sunk-the-*Titanic* is going to be busy so-called rocking on-stage all night with his band. Otherwise we'd have to spend the night surgically removing his arm from your shoulders."

Ira Berg? Who was he? I realized that he had also magically disappeared from my mind the past hour. Why wasn't I dreading the dance and thinking about my mom and dad? Why was I so psyched that I looked good? And why couldn't I wait to get to the dance?

Claude.

After being incredibly stressed out for months, I recognized immediately that he'd made me feel better. He was the first person to make me feel like I wasn't coming from planet Whatever.

But he was going to be there with another girl. Hadn't he said he'd been drafted? Well, since he'd talked about her like she was the army, he couldn't be that psyched about her. Could he?

"Earth to Liza," Serena said, and I realized she was poking me on the shoulder.

"Oh, sorry. I was just thinking about something. Something I want to do over Christmas break."

"What's that?" she asked. "Try to get those last forty points on your SATs? Just for fun?"

I bonked her on the arm. "I wanna relax," I told her, and she beamed in relief. But what I really meant was that there was someone I want to get to know during our ten-day vacation. Someone very, very cool.

Five

Claude

"SURPRISE!"

All of the Trauths were standing around the living-room couch, waving at me as I came down the stairs. I looked around. "Did I miss something?"

"Now, this really isn't a surprise party, son," Mr. Trauther said, grinning widely. "You two boys have to get to that dance! But we did want to give you a little gift of appreciation, and Tom didn't think he could keep himself from telling you anymore."

"A gift?" I said. "A gift for what?"

Mrs. Trauth's eyes were shining. "You've been such a lovely guest and such a great influence on Tom," she announced. Tom groaned. "Hush. It's true. And Claude, we've really come to think of you as one of the family."

I was a little choked up. "I feel like you're my family too," I heard myself saying.

"All right, don't get all weepy on us now, Ma," Tom said. "Claude, this is for you."

It was a square, almost hand-sized box. I looked up at the Trauths, who smiled at me, then opened the gift quickly. Inside was an expensive camera lens.

"It's for your camera at home," Tom said. "Because I remember you saying you used to take pictures with your dad . . ."

I couldn't speak. Even though I felt like I had been in my own world since my arrival, Tom had clearly been listening very carefully. He'd given me a very meaningful gift.

I hadn't even looked at my camera since my father had died, but this made me feel—a little—like I could open it up and take pictures again.

"It's incredible," I managed to say. "I'll never be able to thank you for taking me into your home. . . ." I let the sentence trail off.

"Well, just say you'll take little Terence over for his teenage years," Mr. Trauth boomed. Tom grinned, then made a clown face.

Oh no. I knew what was coming. That singularly American experience, made even more extreme by the Trauths' combined Amazonian size: the group hug. But this time it wasn't so bad.

Since I'd come home from my jog all sweaty, I'd already showered and gotten dressed in the one suit I'd brought with me. Tom rushed upstairs to get ready. He came down wearing a nice suit, which surprised

183

me until I remembered he was dressing up for Liza.

Liza.

Mrs. Trauth made us assemble in the living room for pictures. "All right, everybody say cream cheese!" she boomed.

Click! We all blinked, then smiled again. I couldn't believe that in my short life, I had found my way into this strange, wonderful living room or that I was going to have to leave all these people so soon—these people who'd made me a part of their family as easily as Mrs. Trauth clicked her frosty fingernail on the shutter of her Instamatic.

"Cream cheese!" *Click!*

I thought about seeing my mother again. By tomorrow night I'd be back in our own apartment, telling her about my time in school, and maybe soon showing her pictures I had taken with my great new lens.

"Cream cheese!" *Click!*

"So, Claude," Tom whispered. "Should I give Liza a kiss on the cheek when we meet her in front of the cafeteria?"

The fist landed squarely in my stomach.

Liza, the beautiful girl who I'd been worshiping from afar, was now someone I knew I could talk to. Someone I wouldn't have to hide my feelings from. I wouldn't have to pretend everything was okay when it wasn't.

But my very good friend, a friend for life, liked her. He was the one who'd had the guts to ask her to the dance, and she'd accepted.

I liked her all the more for having the good taste to say yes to Tom and no to that big-pants jerk Ira Berg. At least I could dance vicariously with Liza and be happy for Tom instead of having to hold myself back from drowning Ira face first in a big vat of punch.

"Cream cheese!" *Click!*

"Kissing Liza hello is definitely a good idea," I told him, swallowing the lump in my throat. "On the cheek, though."

Six

Liza

"I JUST CAN'T get over you girls!" Serena's mom kept exclaiming while taking our pictures with her new digital camera. "I only wish your young men were here for the photographs."

Serena groaned loudly. "Moooooooooooooom," she exhaled. "How many times do I have to tell you? I'm a modern woman. I make my own rules. I make my own events. I don't need a date to have a good time at a dance. I'm going solo."

"No one asked, huh?" Serena's mom said with a quick wink at me. "What's wrong with boys today?"

"They're scared," I offered.

"But Liza," Mrs. Waters cut in, clicking away and putting our arms and legs in various poses, "didn't you say *you* had a date? Who's your young man again?"

"Tom Trauth," I replied. "But that's different because we don't like each other that way. We're just going as friends."

"Tom!" exclaimed Serena's mom. "What a darling boy!"

"For your information," Serena announced, teeth clenched, *"three* boys asked me to the dance! Three whole boys! Mmmkay?"

"And you said no to every one of them?" her mother asked, staring at her.

"Well, the guy I sort of like wasn't one of the ones who asked," Serena said, staring at the floor.

Serena liked someone? Why hadn't she told me? Weren't we best friends?

Then again, I'd never told her I thought Claude was cute, and I'd thought so for three months.

"Who is it?" I was dying to know. "I mean, if you want to tell," I added, noticing her smile had faded.

Her mom and I both stared at her. Serena adjusted her tank top, smoothed her hair, and shot us a dazzling smile.

"I'll tell you later tonight, depending on how things go," she told us. "This is gonna be a very interesting night."

Serena and I arrived at the dance to find Tom and Claude waiting by the entrance to the cafeteria. Tom looked great for Tom. He was actually wearing a nice suit, black and normal and everything. Not nerdy at all. And Claude—I think my breath caught in my throat as we walked up to them. He looked *amazing*.

"Omigod!" Serena exclaimed, staring at Tom. "I can't believe I'm looking at the Trauther!"

"We can't *always* all look like we just stepped out of Delia's catalog, now, can we?" Tom shot back.

Serena was struck speechless, which, believe me, was really hard to accomplish.

The four of us were standing face-to-face, like two sets of twins, when all of a sudden Claude leaned very close and whispered in my ear.

"I hope you don't mind," he said. "But Tom asked me to do it first to make sure he doesn't mess it up."

"Do what?" I whispered back, but Claude had already stepped back. He made a deep bow, then took my hand and kissed it gently. I felt an electric tingle down to my toes, as if I suddenly had become the forty-watt bulb on my bedside lamp. Claude took another short bow and then stepped back.

Tom was whooping and clapping. "Boy, I wish I was born in Belgium. That's where he learned that," he remarked to Serena.

"Well, aren't you going to greet your date properly?" Serena smirked at Tom. Claude and I were still looking at each other, but we both snapped out of it at her words.

Tom, I had to remember, was my *date,* and Claude was about to go off and join whoever was his. Still, dancing now seemed like it might be fun—and not just as protection to ward off the evil Ira Berg.

Speak of the devil. The moment I thought his

name he appeared, a small amp in one arm, a carnation in the other.

"Wilde," he whispered, looking me up and down in that sleazy way of his. "You. Look. Hot."

Tom minced up to him, then put his chin in his hand and fluttered his eyelashes. "Is that for me?" he said, snatching the carnation out of his hand. "You *shouldn't* have."

Ira looked from Tom to me, then shrugged. "Out of my way, maggot," he snarled, knocking Tom away with his shoulder so that he crashed into the cafeteria door.

"Well, this is the last time I ever accept a gift from you, Ira Berg!" Tom yelled after him, rubbing his shoulder.

"Yeah, and big spender too, Berg!" Serena shouted. "That carnation must have cost, like, a minute-and-a-half's salary from the Bowlarama." She threw the flower up in the air, and then she and Tom immediately burst into laughter as they took turns smashing it with their feet.

"Two of a kind," Claude said, looking at me sheepishly.

I crossed my arms. "Don't you have to find your date?" I asked. I didn't want to get too caught up in conversation when he was about to walk off with someone else into the "Mardi Gras" night.

Claude looked confused. "A date? I don't have a date."

No date? "But I thought you said you'd been drafted for the dance."

Claude smiled as a look of understanding dawned on his face. "Drafted! Oh yes. That was by Tom." He grinned.

His accent gave me almost the same feeling as having him kiss my hand. "By *Tom*," I repeated.

"To be like . . . his . . . how do you say it? Right something?"

I giggled. It was funny how I could always understand Claude even though languages were my worst subject. "Right-hand man?" I asked.

Claude smiled. "Yes! Exactly! Thank you." Then he darted a quick glance at Tom, as if he wanted to make sure he hadn't heard that. But Tom was busy telling Serena a joke about a talking lizard, and Serena was actually laughing.

I had looked back at Claude, suddenly feeling shy, when Tom grabbed my hand and said, "C'mon, kids! Let's get jiggy with it!"

I gave him back a friendly squeeze, though most of my attention was still focused on Claude, who had offered his arm to Serena.

"Right this way, mademoiselle," Tom said, doing an imitation Groucho Marx with an imaginary cigar. I could hear the opening strains of the Xenophobic Linguistics' favorite crowd pleaser, "Twinkie Romance," as we entered the crowded cafeteria. Whatever else you could say about Ira Berg, he was a really good musician.

"Hey, Liza," Tom said. "You wouldn't mind taking the first dance with Claude, would you? I'd better watch first, get the moves down, then try to boogie so I don't step on your toes."

Mind? I could scarcely believe my good luck! But I didn't want to make Tom feel bad.

"Sure, Tom," I said. "Just as long as you promise not to spend the whole dance in mortal fear of my company."

Tom took both my hands and gave them a big, smacking kiss as he steered me over toward Claude, who was translating all the French on the wall banners for Serena. "That's how we *Americans* do it," Tom explained.

I liked the Belgian way of kissing hands much better.

Seven

Claude

I'D BARELY RECOVERED from the sight of Liza in that incredible red dress when guilt struck for kissing her hand. But Tom had all but forced me to do it, to show him the French way.

I'd been sure I'd leaned too close to her. And when I'd pressed my lips against her soft skin, she had such an awkward look on her face that I'd been convinced I'd completely, as you say here, freaked her out. It's not like anyone went around kissing girls' hands in *any* country.

"Hey!" Ira Berg yelled into the mike on the stage. "We're going to do a very special song. It's called 'Born to Be Wiiiild.'" Looking straight at Liza, he gave a special guitar riff so everyone in the cafeteria would be sure to know *exactly* who he was thinking about if they hadn't picked up on his subtle hints already.

"Primo Jerkdog, huh?" Serena asked.

I didn't understand her except for the word *jerk,* but since it was especially negative, I heartily nodded my agreement.

About twenty feet away, Liza and Tom were close in conference. Suddenly he leaned down and gave both her hands two big, smacking kisses, wiping his mouth with an exaggerated gesture afterward while Liza threw back her head and laughed. I squared my shoulders. I had to make sure this one worked out for Tom.

"They make a cute couple, don't they?" I asked Serena.

Serena looked at me with her eyebrows raised. "A couple of what?"

Oh no! Tom was steering Liza in my direction and waggling his eyebrows in some strange signal that I didn't understand. But I was sure it would involve my getting close to Liza again—and having to somehow conceal my volcanic feelings beneath the surface.

"Claude, I asked Liza if she'd mind dancing with you first so I could watch your moves and copy 'em. It's okay with her. Since poor Serena's here stag, I could keep her company while she doesn't dance."

Serena punched Tom on the shoulder so hard, he flew backward. Tom shot up grinning and flashed me the go-ahead gesture with his thumbs.

"Um, shall we?" I asked Liza, taking her hand.

Out on the dance floor I wasn't surprised to see that Liza was a graceful and funky dancer. But I was surprised to find that dancing with her, I felt relaxed enough to really let loose.

"Tu es un tres bon danseur," Cecily Vaughn said in a mangled French accent as she and Mason Parker danced past.

"Go, Claude!" Serena yelled from the side.

The drummer was doing some long ending solo. I hoped it would go on forever.

Suddenly I felt a shove from the side. "Outta the way, Euro," Ira hissed. "I'm cutting in."

Liza bumped Ira so hard with her hip that he went flying into the couple dancing next to us. Liza cracked up, and I couldn't contain my own laughter.

She took my arm, pulling me close. I couldn't believe it. But I knew it was just to stop that wretched Ira from trying again.

Ira stood there stupidly, glaring at me while we gyrated.

"Yo, Berg! We need you back up here!" someone yelled from the stage.

Ira gave me a dirty look and stomped away.

Liza released me immediately. "Sorry about that." She smiled. "I know you didn't sign up to be Berg repellent."

I was still reeling from her beautiful perfume and the momentary feel of her long, dark hair. "No, I—I enjoyed it—really," I stuttered. That didn't sound good! "I mean, I didn't mind it at all."

Liza smiled again. "Where's Tom?" she asked, glancing around the bodies.

Tom! Of course she wanted to dance the next

one with her date. I looked around the room. "I don't see him *anywhere*," I said. I truly didn't. And with his red hair and trademark fooling around, Tom was pretty easy to spot.

"Some date!" Liza said, smiling.

"Well, don't worry," I told her, feeling a guilty rush of gladness that Tom was nowhere to be found. At least I had had the chance to dance with Liza and to talk with her a while. "I am his right-hand man, after all."

Yeah, and I'd better remember that.

We started swaying to the beat and ended up dancing the next three dances, fast ones. Liza asked me question after question the whole time, about Belgium, about my parents, about the school I'd be going back to for the rest of the term.

"It was really just a bunch of jerks with cell phones and drivers to take them to school and back," I explained, a little out of breath.

"Well, here it's just a bunch of jerks with big pants and AOL accounts," Liza said.

I was surprised to discover how funny Liza was because in school she had always looked so serious. But I got the sense that there was a lot more to learn about Liza. I wanted to know everything about her right now.

"So, Tom told me you take pictures?" Liza said.

When had Tom had time to tell her about that? "I used to," I said. "I'm psyched about starting again."

"It's great to love doing something. I don't

know what I'd do without tennis—probably go crazy."

Suddenly the crowds parted and Tom appeared, carrying two punch glasses. "Hey, Claude! Hey, Liza! Take these, will you?" Tom handed over the glasses, then disappeared back into the crowd, yelling over his shoulder, "I told Serena I'd get her one, so see you in a bit."

Liza watched him run off, then shook her head. "Do you think I did something to offend him?" she asked.

"No way—you know Tom," I offered lamely. "He's probably just nervous, that's all. He's usually the joker type."

But I was having a hard time figuring it out myself. The poor guy must be quaking in his shiny new shoes if he was avoiding his dream date like the plague.

I knew he figured she was safe with me.

Yeah, safe with a guy falling in love with his date.

I swallowed hard.

"Um, so, it's too bad I'm leaving for Belgium tomorrow," I said, figuring I should change the subject since she was obviously upset about getting ditched by Tom.

She stared at me. I couldn't even begin to describe her expression. It was sort of like the one all those teenage actresses had on their faces in the horror-movie trailers.

You idiot! I yelled at myself. *She thinks you're*

hitting on her! She must be majorly horrified at the thought of her date's best friend making a play for her. And really grossed out at the thought.

I gazed helplessly at her, unsure of what to say. Suddenly she looked angry. Really angry. So I guessed it was a combination of both. She thought I was a sleaze, and I grossed her out!

"I—," I began, not even knowing what I'd say.

But she turned and ran out the gym door, her hand covering her mouth.

Eight

Liza

YOU'D THINK AFTER all this time, I would have
learned my lesson? Not to trust people? Not
to open up to them and get interested in their lives?
And most of all not to ever, ever get used to having
them around?

"Hey . . . Liza?" a soft voice asked.

Rubbing some of the dampness from my eyes, I
turned around expecting to see Tom. I could just
kill him! This was all his fault for leaving me alone
with Claude.

How could I have known that in the space of
just one day, I was going to fall for him completely?

It was Claude.

"I'm really sorry about before." He knelt down
next to me. "I didn't mean to offend you or anything. . . ."

Offend me? What was he talking about?

"I—I just—" he said, stumbling over his words. "I mean, um, I just meant it's too bad I'm leaving tomorrow, just when we became friends."

I already knew what he meant. But why would he think I was offended by that? Heart shredded to bits was more like it. Why else did he think I made a total fool of myself by running out of the dance?

"I'm really sorry!" he continued, looking more and more pained as I didn't say anything. "It's just that—that—I know it sounds clichéd, but it's been so long since I've met someone I could really talk to, and—"

"Claude," I said. "Stop. Please." He was being too nice, too apologetic, and I didn't want to burst into tears in front of him. Talk about added humiliation.

He looked at me, then quickly downcast his eyes. "I'm really sorry, Liza," he mumbled. "I'll leave you to yourself now."

"Claude," I burst out. "Wait!"

It wasn't like me to just come out with what I was feeling, but I couldn't help it. I felt like I was going to overflow like a glass of soda if I didn't tell him how disappointed I was that he was leaving tomorrow. And the idea of telling him didn't feel terrible, like yelling at my mom and dad about the divorce or complaining to Serena. It just felt true.

"Claude," I said. He had turned around and was standing in silhouette in front of the cafeteria windows.

"I'm listening," he said, sounding very serious.

"I didn't leave because I was mad at you or offended or anything." *Okay, Liza, that was a good start. Keeping going.*

Claude took a couple of steps toward me. "You didn't?" he asked.

I swallowed. "No. I was just upset that you're leaving . . . you know, America. *Am* upset, I mean."

Claude sat down next to me on the concrete. "But why?" he asked, looking directly in my eyes.

"Because I've finally met someone I can talk to too," I almost shouted. "I just found you," I added in a whisper, then slapped my hand over my mouth. That had sounded a little too ooey-gooey, maybe. I was humiliating myself more by the second.

And Claude was looking at me with no expression on his face. *He must think I'm the biggest slime in the world,* I realized. *Here I am, his best friend's date, and I'm making it loud and clear I'm into him instead.*

My stomach started twisting, and I figured I'd better try to explain in the right way so he wouldn't run off and remember me as a creep.

"It's just that ever since my parents announced their divorce, I've felt like the rug keeps getting pulled out from under me." I sighed. "So, now that we just, um, got to be friends, the last thing I wanted to hear was that you're out of here tomorrow."

"But, Liza," Claude said. "There's e-mail, and letters, and the phone. We can keep in touch—if you want, that is."

"You mean you want to?" I asked. Having him sit so close to me was making me slightly dizzy.

Claude grasped my hands, and it was so comforting, I almost did burst into tears. "Of course I do! You're the first person I've been able to say more than three words to about my dad. It's so easy to talk to you, Liza."

I almost melted. "So you'll e-mail me once you get all settled at home?"

Claude began to swing our hands together back and forth. "I might even swipe one of my classmates' cell phones," he joked.

I felt like a great weight had been lifted. He obviously didn't think I'd been hitting on him. He had no idea I was crazy about him. "Don't go that far," I kidded back. "I don't want to be responsible for leading you into a life of crime."

"Liza, seriously," Claude said, looking somber again. "Change is really hard. Losing things is really hard. But then you end up realizing that you've changed too, grown—as sappy as that sounds—learned how to deal with stuff."

His expression changed, and I knew he was thinking about his dad and himself. "And even though it doesn't take away the hurt," he continued, "sometimes change can also bring good things into your life. It can be really cool to realize you're suddenly a different person than you were."

I held his gaze, then glanced down at my dress and shoes. That was exactly how I'd felt earlier, when I was getting ready for the dance. But I'd thought feeling like a new person was only a cover for how horrible I really felt inside.

But then I realized I hadn't felt so horrible inside when I was at Serena's. I'd felt a million pounds lighter.

Because change had brought a good thing into my life. And maybe I was becoming a new Liza.

I squeezed his hand.

Nine

Claude

LOOKING AT LIZA in the moonlight, with her tear-streaked, lovely face, it was almost impossible not to kiss her right then. But I couldn't do that to Tom—and I couldn't overstep the bounds with Liza just because she wanted to be friends and I wanted to be more.

"Do you want to go find your date?" I asked.

Liza looked confused for a second. "Oh, Tom!" she said, then gave me her arm. "Yeah, we'd better go."

Don't make it more than it is, Delpy, I said to myself as we walked through the cafeteria's heavy double doors into the rocking beat of one of those Xeno— . . . Xeno—whatever—istics songs.

Liza stood up on her toes, trying to see over the crowd. Scanning the room, she suddenly grabbed my arm and pointed at a dim corner near the pushed-up bleachers. "Is *that* him?" she asked, craning her neck to see.

"I'll go get him," I said to Liza. "Wait here."

I wanted to talk to Tom alone, to tell him that I didn't think I could spend any more time with Liza alone, no matter how nervous he was. I wanted to explain to him that she was probably getting the wrong idea, that she thought he didn't like her so much after all.

I'd leave out from my little speech that I'd fallen hopelessly, irrevocably in love.

It *was* Tom in the corner, sitting on some rolled-up mats and hunched over so I couldn't see his face. As I got closer, I realized he was holding Terry's Game Boy, playing a furious game of Tetris with the chemistry crowd who'd come stag.

"Tom, *what* are you doing?" I asked in disbelief.

Tom jumped up. "Claude!" he said, then began to wiggle his right foot wildly. "Uh, I think I sprained my ankle when I was—was getting Serena that punch before, so I thought I'd better rest it in the corner," he stammered.

Enough already. I'd never be able to give Tom a quarter of what he'd given me just by being my friend. By listening. But I *could* try to get it through his nervous skull that he didn't have to be scared of Liza or any girl he liked. That he was an amazing guy and he'd do just fine on his own.

"Tom, you've got the prettiest girl in this school waiting to dance with you," I said. "She's been waiting to dance with you *all* night. It's almost like you were trying to turn me into her date or something, and—"

Oh, man.

Lightbulb.

Understanding had hit me so hard, my knees buckled.

Tom opened his mouth as if he were about to launch a defense, then sighed and gave me a goofy grin. Shrugging, he began to laugh.

"What can I say, El Claudo? Guilty as charged."

"So you never had a crush on Liza?" I asked, staring at him. "I mean, from the minute you asked her to the dance?"

"Sorry, Clauderino," Tom said. He nodded in the direction of Serena, who was dancing with some tall senior not far from us. "No offense, but that loudmouth's more my type."

Out of the corner of my eye I saw Liza walk toward Serena, detach her from her partner, then begin to walk toward us, arm in arm. "But Tom, how did you *know*? How could you have known how much I like her?"

"Gimme a break!" He slapped his forehead. "Like I never noticed you two mooning over each other in the hallways all the time, both too idiotic to make a move. It's your last night, Claude. I had to do *something*."

And I'd thought *I* had something to knock into Tom's skull. I was the one with the thick head.

"What do you mean, *you two*?" I asked. "You're not saying you think Liza likes me too?"

"Claude, Claude, Claude." Tom laughed. "So

many accents, so little girl smarts. You don't think she's dragging Serena over here for *my* benefit, do you?"

"But what if she doesn't!" I burst out. "I can't make a fool of myself."

"That, for starters, is your only problem, Claudorama," Tom said. "But to answer your question, let's just say Serena and I did a little note comparing at the beginning of the dance," he went on. "She *knows* Liza. So unless you put on an Ira Berg mask, I think you've got this made in the shade."

"But—"

But Serena and Liza were suddenly standing next to us, both with devilish sparkles in their eyes. "Everything okeydokey over here, boys?" Serena asked, those eyes exaggeratedly wide and innocent. She was wearing a sash draped across her. Most School Spirit, it read. And how. There must have been some kind of ceremony for the Most awards when Liza and I were outside.

"Peachy, darlink," Tom said, tipping an imaginary hat. "Everything okeydokey with you-all?"

Serena shot me a glance. "Okay, that's like way enough of this dopeyness. I think it's time the switcheroo took effect. We've already wasted half the dance!"

"Switcheroo?" both Liza and I said at the same time. "What's that?"

"You'll know it when you see it," Serena howled, grabbing Tom's arm and pulling him off to the dance floor. Liza and I looked at each nervously.

"So we've been taken," Liza said, fighting back a smile.

Suddenly I felt a dash of Tom's faux suavity. "Well, I'm certainly taken with you, Liza," I said with a grin, and offered her my arm. "Shall we dance?"

Liza's eyes glittered, and she curtsied low. "Certainly, sir," she said, pulling us out onto the floor just as a slow dance began.

"Hey!" I suddenly heard. "Hey, Liza!"

Coming toward us like a tank, I realized, was Ira Berg, who'd abandoned his post at the mike. And he was holding the punch bowl, filled with leftover dregs of sherbet and fruity liquid.

"Hey, Euro trash, I thought you'd like a drink while I danced with Liza," Ira said, the punch bowl balanced on one hand.

I tried to pull Liza behind me, but she wouldn't budge. "Oh, Ira, you incredible jerk," I heard her mutter.

Suddenly there was a *kerplop,* and the punch bowl went up in the air. Ira went flying, face first, into a pool of wet goo. Standing right in front of him was Serena, her foot still stuck out strategically to trip him, a triumphant handful of bead necklaces in her hand.

"Girl, gimme some skin!" Tom yelled. "Well done!"

Serena nodded. "Nothing to it."

Ira shot up amidst hoots and catcalls from everyone, pulling his wet pants up high. "Shut up, you guys! I meant to do it!" he yelled as he ran out the door.

"Sorry for that, er, interesting interpretative dance from our lead singer," said the drummer, who had taken center stage. "Here's 'Rock My Peanut Butter.'"

Liza took my hand, then pressed her cheek close to mine. "Let's not even go there," she said.

That was one American phrase I knew. "Fine with me," I told her, swaying to the song, which was actually slow and quite pretty. "I guess Tom's going to have to give up his crush on Kate Winslet," I said.

Liza drew back and looked at me. "Serena wrote a paper on how Kate Winslet heralded a whole new era of strong roles for women!"

I laughed. "I'm not sure Tom was interested in her for her politics, though. . . ."

For a moment we were silent, just swaying to the music. "I can't believe we have to say good-bye so soon," Liza said.

"Well, you could probably wangle a guilt present from your parents, you know, for how badly you've been affected by their split," I told her. "Maybe you could even ask them for a trip to Belgium."

Her smile almost took my breath away. "I just might do that."

"I'll come and get you at the airport," I said, "but I can't promise to have as many balloons as the Trauths did when they came to pick me up."

"Just you would be fine," Liza said. "But how

will it be when we say hello? I mean, I feel like I've known you for years, but we barely know each other!"

"Well, my mother says the French do greetings better," I said, thinking up a little Tom-like scheme of my own.

"Oh yeah?" Liza murmured against my ear. "And how's that?"

Without waiting, I took her soft face in my hands and kissed her cheeks, one at a time, then kissed her lightly on the lips.

"Hey," she said, "I think I could learn to live with just saying hello for a while."

So we did.

Is He Your Perfect Dance Date?

For months you've agonized over finding the perfect dress, the perfect shoes, and the perfect hairstyle. Now comes the hard part—finding the perfect *date*. Does your guy have what it takes to be your ideal date, or will Mr. Perfect turn into Mr. Perfect Nightmare? Take Jake & Jenny's special quiz to find out.

1. After opening your way-too-crammed locker, everything inside comes tumbling out at your feet. The instant this happens, your crush walks by, and he:

A. Glances down at the mess, looks at you, and keeps on walking

B. Stops, smiles, and says he'd love to give you a hand, but he's late for class

C. Immediately bends down to help you gather your things

2. Your idea of a perfect night out with your guy is a picnic for two on a moonlit beach. His ideal date has the two of you:

A. Sitting in his basement, playing his new video game (he lets you go first)

B. Going bowling with all his buds

C. Cuddling at a nighttime concert on the beach

3. While driving you home after school, he puts on the radio and changes stations several times before he finally settles on:

A. Elevator music

B. The song that just happens to be your all-time favorite

C. Music that instantly gives you a headache and makes your ears ring

4. While shopping at the mall with your friends, you run into him and his friends. It's obvious that he hasn't bought anything and you ask him why. He tells you:

   A. He just bought a bunch of cool new clothes online

   B. He doesn't care what he looks like, so what's the point?

   C. He was waiting to go shopping with you to see what you like him in

5. At lunch you spy him sitting in the caf at a table of girls, flirting like crazy. Later you call him on it. He says:

   A. You're right, I was—sorry . . . with a sheepish smile

   B. So?

   C. What table full of girls? I wasn't even in the cafeteria today

6. You've seen him dance at parties. You would best describe his moves as:

   A. A bit sloppy and clumsy—but kind of cute

   B. Smooth and sexy

   C. Convulsive—several people almost called EMS

7. You and your crush are having a great conversation at a party when you need to excuse yourself for a few minutes. When you return, he's:

   A. Right behind you

   B. Asking your best friend about you

   C. In the same spot, with a drink for each of you and a smile

8. He asks you to the school dance at the last-possible moment. You tell him you already have plans, and he replies:

A. So, can't you change your plans?

B. I'm sorry I waited so long to ask you, but will you save me a dance?

C. Oh, well, maybe next time

9. Your crush enters the school talent show to perform:

A. A popular song after inhaling helium

B. A lip sync

C. A song he wrote

10. The night of the dance he picks you up:

A. On time, bearing flowers and looking incredibly cute

B. In a van full of his friends

C. A half hour late with no excuse

SCORING:

1.	A=0	B=1	C=2
2.	A=1	B=0	C=2
3.	A=1	B=2	C=0
4.	A=1	B=0	C=2
5.	A=2	B=1	C=0
6.	A=1	B=2	C=0
7.	A=0	B=1	C=2
8.	A=0	B=2	C=1
9.	A=1	B=0	C=2
10.	A=2	B=1	C=0

The Verdict

If your score is between 0 and 7:

You might be better off going solo or with your friends. You and this guy sound pretty incompatible—fifteen minutes at the dance with him just might send you running out the door . . . on toes he squished by stepping on them all night!

If your score is between 8 and 14:

Okay, so he's not your perfect date, but he does have potential. He just might be worth getting to know a little better, and maybe he'll even turn into Mr. Perfect. Sometimes guys who fall between perfect and perfect nightmare are just shy or even a little nervous. Think about giving Mr. Maybe a chance.

If your score is between 15 and 20:

Looks like you hit the jackpot—he sounds like your kind of guy! You'll dance, laugh, talk, and smile the night away. Hold on to this one—there's a very good chance that your perfect dance date could turn into your Mr. Perfect!

Don't miss any of the books in *Love Stories*
—the romantic series from Bantam Books!

#1 *My First Love* . . . . Callie West
#2 *Sharing Sam* . . . . Katherine Applegate
#3 *How to Kiss a Guy* . . . . Elizabeth Bernard
#4 *The Boy Next Door* . . . . Janet Quin-Harkin
#5 *The Day I Met Him* . . . . Catherine Clark
#6 *Love Changes Everything* . . . . ArLynn Presser
#7 *More Than a Friend* . . . . Elizabeth Winfrey
#8 *The Language of Love* . . . . Kate Emburg
#9 *My So-called Boyfriend* . . . . Elizabeth Winfrey
#10 *It Had to Be You* . . . . Stephanie Doyon
#11 *Some Girls Do* . . . . Dahlia Kosinski
#12 *Hot Summer Nights* . . . . Elizabeth Chandler
#13 *Who Do You Love?* . . . . Janet Quin-Harkin
#14 *Three-Guy Weekend* . . . . Alexis Page
#15 *Never Tell Ben* . . . . Diane Namm
#16 *Together Forever* . . . . Cameron Dokey
#17 *Up All Night* . . . . Karen Michaels
#18 *24/7* . . . . Amy S. Wilensky
#19 *It's a Prom Thing* . . . . Diane Schwemm
#20 *The Guy I Left Behind* . . . . Ali Brooke
#21 *He's Not What You Think* . . . . Randi Reisfeld
#22 *A Kiss Between Friends* . . . . Erin Haft
#23 *The Rumor About Julia* . . . . Stephanie Sinclair
#24 *Don't Say Good-bye* . . . . Diane Schwemm
#25 *Crushing on You* . . . . Wendy Loggia
#26 *Our Secret Love* . . . . Miranda Harry
#27 *Trust Me* . . . . Kieran Scott
#28 *He's the One* . . . . Nina Alexander
#29 *Kiss and Tell* . . . . Kieran Scott
#30 *Falling for Ryan* . . . . Julie Taylor
#31 *Hard to Resist* . . . . Wendy Loggia
#32 *At First Sight* . . . . Elizabeth Chandler
#33 *What We Did Last Summer* . . . . Elizabeth Craft
#34 *As I Am* . . . . Lynn Mason
#35 *I Do* . . . . Elizabeth Chandler
#36 *While You Were Gone* . . . . Kieran Scott
#37 *Stolen Kisses* . . . . Liesa Abrams
#38 *Torn Apart* . . . . Janet Quin-Harkin
#39 *Behind His Back* . . . . Diane Schwemm
#40 *Playing for Keeps* . . . . Nina Alexander
#41 *How Do I Tell?* . . . . Kieran Scott

SUPER EDITIONS

Listen to My Heart . . . . Katherine Applegate
Kissing Caroline . . . . Cheryl Zach
It's Different for Guys . . . . Stephanie Leighton
My Best Friend's Girlfriend . . . . Wendy Loggia
Love Happens . . . . Elizabeth Chandler
Out of My League . . . . Everett Owens
A Song for Caitlin . . . . J.E. Bright
The "L" Word . . . . Lynn Mason
Summer Love . . . . Wendy Loggia
All That . . . . Lynn Mason
The Dance . . . . Craig Hillman, Kieran Scott, Elizabeth Skurnick

Coming soon:

#42 His Other Girlfriend . . . . Liesa Abrams

You'll always remember your first love.

Love Stories

Looking for signs he's ready to fall in love?

Want the guy's point of view?

Then you should check out *Love Stories*. Romantic stories that tell it like it is—why he doesn't call, how to ask him out, when to say good-bye.

Love Stories

Available wherever books are sold.